I0533602

OUT OF THE BARREL

Also, by Lawrence Christopher:

Mick Hart Mysteries

All About Mary
Mary's Little Lamb
Dog 'Em

Other Fiction

Ghettoway Weekend
Later Days and Nights
Out of the Barrel

The Tickle Fingers Children's Books

Where is Pinky?
Five Fingers Prayer Book

Published dozens of short stories online

www.Timbooktu.com.

Out of the Barrel
A novella by
LAWRENCE CHRISTOPHER

UNLIMITED

Atlanta, Georgia
Published by MF Unlimited, Civic Center Station, Box 55346, Atlanta, GA 30308

All rights reserved. No parts of this may be reproduced or transmitted in any form or by any means, electronic or mechanical, including photocopying, recording, or by any information storage and retrieval system, without permission in writing from the publisher. Copyright © 2015 by Michael L. Faulkner. Any similarity to persons living or dead is purely coincidental.

ISBN 10: 0-97122-788-8, ISBN 13: 978-0-9712278-8-0
Printed in the United States of America

Cover Design by I Draw Christian Logos and Tolbert Graphics

Acknowledgments

For all my family and friends who have made it out of the barrel. *Stay up*!

The Characters

Adrian Wiggins – Atlanta, OBGYN Physician Assistant to the stars of RHOA and other locally filmed Reality Shows. Born and raised by his grandmother in the small town of Marion, Indiana. After graduating from high school, he moved to Atlanta, Georgia to attend Morehouse School of Medicine. Adrian is among the finest looking "pretty" men walking the Buckhead streets of The ATL. Women desire him. Men question him. The question is whom Adrian wants.

Deshaun Howard – married with a child, Deshaun is the embodiment of the lyrics to Hip-Hopper, Drake's song "*Started from the Bottom.*" The Albertus-Brown Projects (Odelot, Ohio's oldest public housing complex, was Deshaun's home growing up. His childhood was that of a cliché like many impoverished minorities – he never knew his father and he was raised by a struggling single mother. Deshaun's longtime friend helped him apply to Clark Atlanta University (CAU), from where he graduated and obtained a job as a software engineer for a global technology firm.

Earl Grey –Grammar and high school peers referred to Earl as a bookworm and a nerd. With his book smart, left-handed spurred creative brain, Earl became a rising star in the advertising industry after graduating from CAU with a degree in Mass Media Arts. He walked away at the top of his class and became a Brand Strategist for celebrities and corporate executives. He grew up in a middle-class family home, to become a modest millionaire.

Fiona Antoinette-Setche Tamajong – nicknamed FAST, came to America as a teenager and hit the ground running just like she did on the dirt roads of Cameroon Africa. She went from beating her grammar school male classmates, to being a repeated Cross Country Player of the Week for the Spelman College Jaguars. After graduating from the female HBCU with a double major in Business Administration/Finance, Fiona was hired by a global health and public services consulting firm.

Prologue

It was the happiest day to date of Deshaun Howard's early twenties. Months away from graduating from Clark Atlanta University; Deshaun just received a job offer from NBM (National Business Machine) potentially earning more money than he had ever dreamed of making being an impoverished kid from the Brand Whitlock/Albertus Brown Homes housing projects in Odelot, Ohio. On this day, Deshaun reached the upper rim of the proverbial barrel. He called his girlfriend Vera Diaz as soon as he left the interview, telling her of the good news. Equally excited, she too had some good news she wanted to share, but she said that she would wait until he came home to their shared off-campus apartment.

Later in the day when Deshaun walked in the door of their off-campus apartment on Euharlee Street in Southwest Atlanta, the aroma that greeted him from the kitchen came from *adobo* and *sofrito* -blends of herbs and spices that give many of the Spanish foods their distinctive taste and color. He could see his girlfriend in the kitchen stirring something in a pot on the stove. She was wearing a dress and shoes that he hadn't seen her wear before, and her hairstyle looked different. The high heels made her Puerto Rican posterior lift underneath the snug-fitting dress. He was awe-inspired by the sight.

The dinner table conversation consumed Deshaun recalling the day's event.

"Girl, you should have seen us. We were sitting at a table with white tablecloths in this high-class restaurant. The dude had on this crisp white shirt and dark blue suit and a red tie. He told me to order anything on the menu, so you know I hurt 'em, right. I ordered a T-bone steak with the works, and I *smashed it*. After we ate, he had some coffee and dessert. That's when he made me the offer. I mean it was so cool the way he did it. He pulled out this folded piece of paper from inside his suit coat and slid it across the table. All that was on it was the number fifty-three with a K behind it. He asked me if that was okay with me for my starting salary. I played it cool and took my time before I answered." Deshaun paused to stuff more food in his mouth.

Finally, Vera got the chance to share her good news. But first, she inspected the manicure that she had received earlier in the day. The gold rhinestone trimming on the wild rose-colored gel nail polish was pleasing to her. What she wasn't pleased about, was that Deshaun hadn't said anything about how nice she looked. Then again, she thought if he had noticed her fresh hairdo, new dress, and Aldo pumps; then he might have asked where she got the money to pay for it all.

"*Carifio*, well I had a pretty good day too." Vera proclaimed.

"Oh yeah. What happened?"

"I got some good news from my doctor."

"From your doctor; is something wrong?"

"Oh no, nothing wrong; I just went in for my routine gynecological check-up."

"Okay, so what's the good news then? The *coochie, coochie* is okay, isn't it?"

"Yes, the *coochie* is fine."

"Then *what's up*?

"Well, we're – *Vamos a tener un bebé*." Vera often reverted to speaking Spanish when she wanted to be indirect.

Earlier that day.

"You've *gots* to be *SHITTIN'* me," exclaimed the agitated young man.

"No *baby*, I had it right here in my pocket."

"I told you that was all the money I could hustle up. I ain't got no more."

"I know *baby*. I don't know what happened to it." The even younger girl cried with genuine tears streaming down her cheeks.

"I know you ain't *tryin'* to put me on *lock* for no eighteen years, *is* you?"

"No. No. I wouldn't do that to you. Baby, maybe it's a sign that we shouldn't do this; that we should keep it."

"It's a sign alright. A sign *yo' ass tryin'* to trap me.

"I'm not like that. I love you, *baby*."

"*SHIT!* Come on, let's go look for it."

The upheaval followed the young couple as they left the waiting room of the abortion clinic. A laminated card with the number twelve printed on it remained crumpled in the seat where the young girl sat. Vera looked at the #13 card in her trembling left hand. In her right coat pocket, she clenched in her fist an envelope with $350 in small bills; an envelope that she had found in the parking lot just before entering the clinic.

The glass window slid open at the receptionist's area. "TWELVE," the receptionist loudly beckoned. The grandmother and granddaughter looked to see who would answer the call. So did the two best friends who were holding one another's hands. Sitting alone, Vera knew that the holders of number twelve had gone and soon her number would be called. Rising to her feet grabbing the left behind the number card, she headed to the window. She obverted looking in the direction of the eyes that were on her.

"Is your number twelve," asked the receptionist.

"No." Vera subtly responded while handing the receptionist two laminated cards. She then turned and quickly walked away and out of the clinic's door.

Contents

One - Who Are You With?

"You can't live your life for other people. You've got to do what's right for you, even if it hurts some people you love." – Nicholas Sparks (The Notebook)

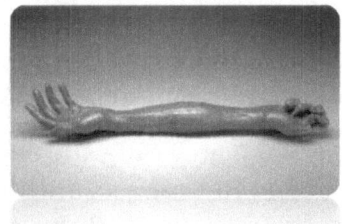

"So you know that my wife's brother is *livin'* with us, right?" Deshaun asked and answered. Earl Grey, his best friend since childhood gave an affirmative nod as he enjoys one of his guilty pleasures of jalapeno stuffed olives and a glass of raisin sherry.

"So this dude asks to borrow my car to go get some beer. He's gone like two hours. I ask him where the hell he's been. He says, 'I was caught up in traffic. You know how it is up at Camp Creek Parkway on the weekend.' First of all, I live thirty minutes from there *and* he be *knowin'* how I complain *'bout* the traffic up there. That's why he came up with that *'scuse.*"

"Sounds like a legitimate reason to be late." Earl offered.

"*Nah,* see you don't understand. He didn't have to go all the way up there for no damn beer."

"Why not? I drive from my house to go to that World of Beverage store."

"Yeah, that's because you drink that high-end shit, like you *drinkin'* now."

"Sherry is not high-end."

"You know what I'm *sayin'*. But for a can of two-eleven crap he drinks, he could have stopped at any gas station or package store. That's another thing; his *ass* doesn't ever think about *buyin'* for the house. It's always for him. And he does that shit on purpose, *cuz* he knows I don't drink that crap. He *gonna* tell me the reason he don't buy me any beer is *cuz* Corona cost too much. Bull!"

"De' man, I know you didn't drive across town to complain about your brother-in-law taking a joyride in your Mercedes."

"Yeah, I did. But you right man – not just that. I just needed to get out *da* house. Ever since he moved in, it's been one thing after another. It's been a month now and all he does is lay around *playin'* on my X-box and *watchin'* TV. Me and Vera ain't *hittin' it* as much *cuz* he always around the house."

Earl cringed a bit as he listened to his longtime friend's slippage into his street lingo. He knows it's only because Deshaun is comfortable with him and that they're just hanging out. Growing up, Earl had always been teased as being decorous in his speech. Even as an adult he has been accused of "talking white" because of his proper dialect. As a Brand Strategist, usually working with corporate executives, Earl was assured within himself and how he needed to sound to be successful in his career. He also knew he had cringed when he made Deshaun his project and work in progress.

They met as boys at the Catholic Club, a faith-based childcare and family center serving families of Odelot, Ohio's inner-city neighboring areas. Though they came from different parts of the city, the two youth's paths collided at the deep end of the center's Olympic size swimming pool. It was at that pool where Earl took a brave yet foolish dive off the ten feet high diving board. It was foolish because he didn't know how to swim. He hadn't even learned how to float.

After submerging in the water, Earl quickly realized that his brief time playing in the shallow end of the twenty-foot pool wasn't long enough nor time well spent. There he was after the dive flailing his arms and legs trying to propel himself upward. He only managed to get close enough to the surface to see the lifeguard and others standing by the poolside. Earl began screaming for help, but his call was drowned out by a mouth full of chlorinated water. His tears for fear of drowning were washed away.

Finally, Earl gave up. He made his peace with God for the short life he had lived up to the age of ten. For all the fibs he had told his mother – for the roll of butterscotch Lifesavers he stole from the A&P Market - and for the time he took the Sears store catalog up to his bedroom so that he could look at the women modeling nothing but bras and panties - he was sorry. God heard his cry of repentance and sent an angel to save him.

Along swam Deshaun completely oblivious of Earl's listless body just beneath him. It must have been the thrashing of Deshaun's strokes that alerted Earl of his presence. In a desperate and last ditched effort, Earl lunged toward the swimmer and grabbed ahold of him. Caught unaware, Deshaun tried to fight off his attacker. He pushed him. He punched him. They wrestled. Like the biblical Jacob held on to the angel, Earl would not let go.

"HE'S TRYIN' TO KILL ME," Deshaun yelled; as he broke the surface of the water.

The lifeguard jumped into the pool and managed to separate the two boys, taking Earl safely to the poolside. Earl cared little about the reprimand he received from the lifeguard. It went in one ear and washed out the other. What did matter to him was the boy who saved his life and the best friendship that began that day.

Although Deshaun lived near the west side of Odelot and Earl in the Old Town End portion of the inner city, their paths would cross again. Academics brought the two together at the University of Odelot. Earl was an inductee of the Odelot EXCEL scholarship incentive program for B average students, while Deshaun was enrolled in another college preparatory program called Upward Bound for C average schoolchildren. Both programs served targeted groups traditionally underrepresented in higher education. The students were tutored in their high school courses, took college courses, traveled in, out, and around the country, attending annual summer academic institutes, all while having to maintain passing grade levels. Deshaun needed a little more personal tutoring, which Earl was happy to oblige giving to the boy who saved his life. Deshaun was more streetwise than the school of street hustling. He abided by the rule: "if you don't play the game, then the game plays you."

The boy's steps were ordered for common ground; their backgrounds couldn't be more different. The Howards were three generations surviving on government assistance and living in project housing. Deshaun Howard's mother was a stay-at-home single mom with a side hustle of being the "Candy Lady," selling bootleg snacks out of their two-bedroom apartment. She made frequent appearances in the publication *Buckeyes Behind Bars* with the disclaimer: "All individuals in our publications are innocent until proven guilty by a court of law..." Deshaun secretly collected each edition his mother appeared.

"So, what you're really upset about is that his being in your house is interfering with your sex life."

"Nah. Yeah. Maybe. I mean; he's just one of those *in the world brothers;* you know *nuttin-to-dos.* He's about nothing."

"Listen, what you need to do is set a timeframe for how long he's going to be allowed to stay with you. Give him say, three or four months."

"I don't know if Vera will go *fo'* that."

"You guys need to talk it over and be in agreement on it. Otherwise, he'll just play one of you against the other like a child would do its parents."

"I mean, it is her brother and all."

"And who invited him to come and stay in the first place?"

"She did."

"Without discussing it with you?"

"Well, she told me the day before she went to pick him up from the Greyhound bus station."

"De', you have a bigger problem than your brother-in-law in your house. Your mother-in-law is also living in your house. But to stay on point about him – if you let him get too comfortable, at some point he may start to lose respect for you. It may start with borrowing without asking to outright 'I'm taking this.'"

"I hear you, man. You right - you right. Vera and I need to talk."

Earl's mobile phone rang. The name Adrian Wiggins flashed on the phone's display.

"Hold up," Earl stated. "It's Adrian," he informed Deshaun.

"I don't know 'bout yo' boy."

"What do you mean?"

"The last time we were *hangin'* out, you know he asked me how he looked in some jeans he just bought." Deshaun shook his head.

"He what?"

"He asked me how he looked in *dem* jeans, like some chick."

Earl chuckled out loud as he slid his finger across the phone's display to answer the call. "Talk to me," requested Earl of his caller.

"*What it do*, Earl?" Adrian Wiggins was in trying to be in a cool mode.

"Nothing much. Just talking with Deshaun."

"Yeah, tell '*im* I said '*what'sup*.'"

"Will do. So, what's up with you?"

"I was wondering when you're going to work out?"

"Tomorrow morning."

"That works. Wanna hook up?"

"Sure."

"Your place or mine?"

"Mine."

"*Aight*; see you there at six-thirty," Adrian confirmed.

Two - Work It Out.

"Exercise strengthens the body. Reading sharpens the mind. Prayer tempers the spirit. Live a balanced life." – Bishop Dale C. Bronner

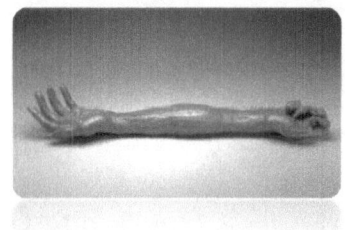

The up-tempo music was playing in the Snap Fitness gym for the early morning risers who made it in for workouts. The muted television was showing the local news. Newscasters were tag-teaming in presenting the litany of overnight crimes and developments. Gym patrons were on the myriad of training equipment in efforts to slim down, tone up, add muscle, or lose weight. *Earl* and *Adrian* were in the cardio room stretching and warming up.

"Have you heard the latest about Kobe, and him suing his mother?" Adrian asked.

"No." Earl shook his head hoping to indicate that he didn't care.

"Yeah, she's supposed to be trying to sell some of his memorabilia and he's trying to stop her. On top of that, she's supposed to be struggling, while he's got his in-laws living pretty well. At least that's what they're saying." Adrian provided.

Adrian was the only guy that Earl knew whose primary source of news came from gossip tabloids and such. His sources were *TMZ,*

BOSSIP, *Necole Bitchie's type* online blogs, or straight from the patients' mouths at the OBGYN office where he's a Physician Assistant.

"One, it's his money to do with it as he pleases. Two, what makes him responsible for taking care of his mother?" Earl gave in Kobe's defense.

"Look who's talking . . . the man who took his mother on a vacation trip to Cancun."

"And what's wrong with that?"

"A single, good-looking guy doesn't go on an exotic vacation with his mother."

"This one does; plus that's totally different than me taking care of her." Earl shot back in his defense.

Though, Adrian was unaware that Earl had bought his mother a house in the suburbs of Odelot, Ohio away from where he was raised in the inner city. He also bought her a brand-new Chrysler 300 sedan for her birthday.

In Earl's next breath, "That's why we can't get ahead. While many of us who *made* it believe that everyone we grew up with and our family is entitled to share in what we've worked hard for."

"What, you don't believe in giving back?"

"I believe begging family members in *getting back* when it comes to them wanting to help me spend my money," Earl spoke venomously, recalling his last conversation with his mother who wanted him to buy her the latest announced iPhone. He was already carrying her on his phone plan where she constantly would overrun their data plan because she would forget to log on to Wi-Fi while she watched downloaded episodes of her favorite television shows.

"So, if you won the lottery, you wouldn't give any money to your mother?"

"I wouldn't give her a dime, directly." Earl clarified.

"What, you would set up a trust fund or something for your mother?"

"Nope. I'd hire a financial planner to handle paying off her debt. Clean up and bring current everything on her credit reports. That way, her very next paycheck is hers to do with it as she pleases."

"And what if she didn't want you and your planner all up in her business?"

"Oh well."

Adrian wasn't convinced that Earl would be as callous when it came to helping his mother as he claimed. Based solely on the knowledge that Earl takes his mother on his vacation trips; he felt that the man had a generous heart and spirit. Adrian was envious of Earl's relationship with his mother, because of his estranged relations with his mother and family.

Thinking back on his childhood growing up in Marion, Indiana; Adrian was the product of a biracial union. His mother Helen Wiggins was Caucasian, and his father was a native of the Dominican Republic. He never knew his father; he just knew of him. What he heard of his father sounded much like the literary character Johnny Appleseed. Like Johnny, Adrian's father was known for randomly spreading his seed everywhere he went.

Adrian was a pretty-looking baby, olive skin tone, with light-colored eyes, and a head full of curly black hair. He had multiethnic features, which prompted the box on his birth certificate to be checked as "Other." His only discernible feature from his father's lineage was a sizeable penis. Only days old he'd been given the nickname "Pinkie" after attending nurses in the maternity ward would jokingly compare his manhood to their pinkie fingers. Eventually, the nickname got back to Adrian's mother. Seeing the organ herself made her smile as she thought of the pleasures that his father's penis had brought her.

Helen had mixed emotions about her born out of wedlock son's ethnicity. At the time of Adrian's conception and birth, interracial dating wasn't the fad or trending event that it had later become in their small town. In Marion, the population of about 30,000, where African Americans made up fifteen percent of the population and Hispanics and other groups had moved into the city at a large rate.

Helen's pretty baby grew into a good-looking boy, and she enjoyed the attention he brought from the women fawning over him. Even with that attention, it didn't overcome the negative gossip about the bastard half-breed child. There still was an older generation of whites that saw the darker hue of Adrian and looked upon him as a bastard black child to a white girl who was taken advantage of and abandoned by a black man. To right what she perceived as a societal wrong, Helen married Parker Mason, a white man, a school superintendent. Together they had a child.

Despite the wedding vows, Parker did not mean it when he vowed: "to cherish and respect you, to care and protect you, to comfort and encourage you, and stay with you, for all eternity." He did not respect nor fully accept Adrian's mother for having a child out of wedlock, let alone by a man of another race. Parker Mason faked his acceptance of Adrian for about a year after his stepsister was born. At the age of six, Adrian was given over to his Busia (grandmother in Polish) to be raised. His mother was heartbroken but wanted to hold on to her husband, the father of her daughter, and to keep some portion of her new family intact.

Three - Who's Who?

Quick question: How can anyone ever love you for who you are if you become someone else to be with them?

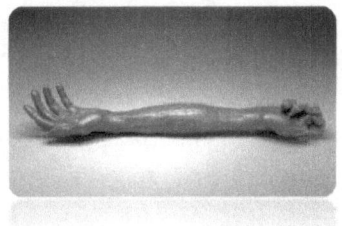

*The Atlanta Falcons were once again going to the NFL Playoffs. The diehard **Falcon's** fans in and about the north Georgia city were celebrating the reprieve from an early ending season. The **team's Pro Bowl** wide receiver, Raymond "RR" Royce hosted his celebration party in his luxurious Lithonia, Georgia home. For Raymond, there was more cause for celebration than the professional football team that he played for making it to **postseason** play. He **had** made a promise to his girlfriend and Falcon's cheerleader, Fiona Tamajong, that if the team made it to the playoffs, they would be engaged to be married.*

It wasn't long after being drafted to the team when RR became the premier receiver on the Falcon's roster, getting his hands on every football thrown in his direction. His pro-bowl performance on the field also managed to easily get his hands on a bevy of beautiful women.

*Fiona arrived at the party fashionably late. She felt this was the pinnacle night of her blessed life. Raised by her parents in Cameroon, Africa until she graduated from middle school. She then moved to the United States to attend **a** high school where she ran relay sprints on the track team which earned her the nickname FAST, which was also* *her monogram. Her performance on the track gained her a scholarship to Spelman College in Atlanta, Georgia. Upon graduating with dual degrees in Human Services and French, Fiona landed a job with a global healthcare company, for which she travels as a consultant. As if her life couldn't get any better; she was chosen as one of the 36 out of 200 women who tried out to be an Atlanta Falcon's cheerleader. Now she had sideline access and opportunity to rich professional athletes.*

Once again, Fiona won out over the multitude of her competitors. On paper, they were viewed as a storybook suitable couple. The prospect of marriage to RR would be the ideal ending to Fiona's Coming to America fairytale.

Making her way through the crowd of partiers, Fiona was in a hurried search of her beau and would-be fiancé. At times she was being deliberately blocked as well as pawed by drunkard male guests at the party. Even some of RR's defensive linemen teammates had their hands in **attempting to block** *her. The first game room* **in the house** *was full of partiers, but no RR. It was not until she made her way to his private entertainment room did, she happens upon Raymond and one of her fellow cheerleaders. Raymond was sprawled on a settee that Fiona helped him select. There he was with his legs gapped while the female kneeling before him, whose head was bobbing. Fiona turned and stormed out of the house screaming obscenities that no one could understand because she was speaking* **Camfranglais;** *a mixture of English, French, and Pidgin.*

Publicly, the relationship between Fiona and RR was over. But it would not be that easy. Throughout their courtship, Raymond Royce convinced Fiona to go into business together as co-owners in a Jamba Juice franchise and a car wash business. Both businesses were in a strip mall in Lithonia near Raymond's home. It was not the best location from a traffic market standpoint. For RR, the location gave him more of a sense of control by having his business nearby and it made for a convincing argument to have Fiona spend nights at his home when she would visit the store. Fiona's Kennesaw, Georgia home was an hour north of Raymond's and she did not like driving in the Atlanta interstate traffic.

Privately, **after the breakup,** Fiona would succumb to the tugs of her heart, and she would occasionally find herself in the grasp of RR's strong and apologetic **receiving** arms. RR would call her to go over some business issues and financial figures. He proudly called himself a devil's man; six **feet two inches** tall, with six-pack abs and a **seven-**figure income. Fiona was weak to the prowess of **an alpha male** - a devil's man. He had a tether on her heart as well as her finances.

RR was a cable television installer before he won a multi-year contract with the professional football team. During the installer days, Fiona helped him improve his credit score by adding him to her credit cards as a rider. He ran the card balances up without paying her. He maintained the empty promises that he would pay the cards off.

As much as she enjoyed being one of the three dozen cheerleaders; Fiona did not re-up for a third season with the squad. Being a full-time Health and Public Service consultant and volunteering in the Atlanta community did not leave her much *me time.* Earning **an upper** five-figure income, she would not miss the small stipend that the Falcons provided for dancing at home games.

Despite the occasional physical dalliances with RR, Fiona was no longer committed to the relationship. She had plenty of would-be suitors who approached her regularly. Whether they were colleagues or clients, offers of **a** request for marriage proposals were copiously extended. She accepted their generosity of dinners, entertainment **shows,** and gift-giving. "It was not like I asked for the **generous** offers," she told herself.

Fiona made a vow not to commit or compromise her integrity **again** with another man. Instead, she would be relationship carefree and deal with men as they come and go. She would remain single until someone came along who complimented her life in a way that made it **and her** better.

৵৵৩৵৵

"'ey *Babe*," Fiona addressed Earl Grey over the Bluetooth Sync in her **Audi sedan**, during the drive on I-285 South from Hartsfield–Jackson Atlanta International Airport.

"Hey yourself." Earl inwardly blushed at hearing the affectionate *Babe* term of endearment that Fiona haphazardly used.

"What are your plans for this weekend?"

"Quite a bit actually. Tomorrow morning I'm volunteering some time with *Back on My Feet*, helping some homeless guys with writing resumes. Then in the evening, the Atlanta Business League is honoring me at their *Men of Influence* ceremony."

"Well aren't you the busy bee. Do you 'ave a date for the dinner?"

"No, I don't. Do you know of someone who might be available?"

"*Oui*. I'll be there after I make a stop to buy an outfit." After disconnecting the call, Fiona remained on the expressway, rerouting to Stonecrest Mall. While she welcomed any opportunity to buy new clothes and shoes, she was looking forward to a quiet weekend at Earl's **Decatur** home as she whispered in her French native tongue; "*la douceur de ne rien faire*" (the sweetness of doing nothing). Just as she settled in for the rest of her drive, Fiona's phone echoed **through the car's speakers**. It was her housemate, Kendra Reynolds.

Kendra and Fiona had been friends since their days as Spelman College dorm roommates. Fiona spoke broken English **when she arrived on campus.** She relied heavily on Kendra to teach her the lay of the land of the **AUC**, to survive her first year at a Historically Black College University.

Fiona was a quick study and was soon managing on her own. Kendra became envious of her Motherland roommate. Fiona was everything boys sought; being attractive, athletic, and exotic looking, and on top of that she was smart. In her own right, Kendra was the girl next door cute and street-smart savvy. Still, she often found herself regaling questions from the guys on campus; "What about your friend."

"*Bonjour*, Kendra," Fiona answered her phone.

"Don't be bonjouring me *heffa*. Where are you?"

"I'm on my way to the mall."

"What mall?"

"Don't you mean *which* mall?"

"Whatever. You funny; when I'm the one who taught yo' ass how to speak. So, which mall?"

"I'm on my way to Stonecrest."

"That means you're over by Earl's."

"*Oui.*"

"So, will you be home this weekend?"

"Maybe, late on Sunday."

"Why don't you just move in with the guy?" Kendra snapped.

As soon as the last word left her mouth, she wished she could pull it back. Fiona moving out was the last thing she wanted to happen. Though they were roomies, technically Kendra was a houseguest. The Kennesaw, Georgia condo and everything associated with it was in Fiona's name. Kendra paid the cable bill now and then and bought groceries mainly to her liking and taste.

The *one-time* college roommates became *roomies* again when Kendra's husband cheated on her and she was asked to move out of their home. When he emptied her belongings from the house *she originally had in her name,* he also emptied the money from their joint bank accounts

When Kendra and her husband were dating, she had good credit and good scores with the three reporting agencies. He was going to a barber's college in pursuit of his dream to open his shop. It was during that time she started charging items on her credit cards for him. It started with laptops, clothes, and plane tickets. After he graduated from college, she took out cash advances on the credit cards and co-signed for a loan to help him open his barbershop.

In a little over a year, she had amassed a two-credit card debt of $12,000 – which she carried over into their marriage expecting him to help pay off the bills. Instead, they continued to accumulate more debt. The money her husband made either went into the business or his pockets.

At the time of the divorce, Kendra's credit score had Raymond below 500 (Bad category range), her credit cards were maxed, and she had no emergency funds saved. Kendra was three days behind on her *next rearranged* monthly car payment. Her lender remotely activated a device in her car's dashboard that prevented her car from starting. Before she could get on the road, she had to pay more than $700, money she did not have. *Frantically, Kendra called Fiona who was working out of town and begged her to send the money to keep the car from being repossessed. Fiona paid on the account via Western Union. An account setup she had arranged to do before.*

"We're going to a dinner tomorrow. I will be 'ome Sunday." Fiona offered.

Kendra abruptly changed the conversation to be about a guy she just met. The discussion lasted while Fiona shopped in and out of mall stores. They would have been on the phone even longer if Fiona had not gotten on an elevator to lose the phone signal. **Fiona** then turned off the phone.

ক্ষক্ষণ্ডঞ

The black-tie "Men of Influence" dinner was a gala event held at the downtown Atlanta Hilton hotel. The men were in traditional formal black-tie attire. The women were in floor-length gowns that fit like **gloves** for smaller size figures. Fiona, on the other hand, went dressed in a thigh-length, lace sheath dress. The style of the dress, helped by four-inch heels, accentuated the roundedness of her rump and her shapely legs.

During the dinner, the men being honored were announced. The list reflected the names of black men in metro Atlanta communities who have reached senior-level positions within their profession, are leading entrepreneurs in their industry, have proven history-making feats, or have attained the ability to influence large public bodies politically and in government. In addition to professional accomplishments, the "Men of Influence" had demonstrated their commitment to the citizenry of Metro Atlanta by maintaining significant involvement and participation in community and civic activities.

Earl was called to the stage. As he stood from the table, Fiona grabbed his hand and, on the back, planted a full lip kiss. This would be the first kiss of many to come before the night would end. After the dinner, there was an after-hours dance. While Earl wanted to leave, Fiona wouldn't have it. She loved to dance, Earl did not. The disc jockey enticed the attendees to the dance floor by opening with Michael Jackson's *Wanna Be Startin' Somethin'*. Fiona saw this as a sign to aid in coaxing Earl onto the dance floor.

"Earl, did you know that ♫ *Ma ma se, ma ma sa, ma ma coo sa*♫ line in this song was originally from Manu Dibango's 'Soul Makossa.' The syllables originate in the language Duala of Cameroon; it means 'let's dance.'" Fiona informed.

"No, I didn't."

"So the song begs that you come dance with me."

"Okay, one dance." Earl conceded.

One dance turned out to be three until the DJ started with the series of group line dance songs, *Electric Slide*, *Cupid Shuffle*, and the *Wobble*. Earl left Fiona to dance, not alone, but with the flurry of women and a few brave men who joined in. Fiona was a natural dancer, and during the *Wobble* she incorporated the Assiko dance moves of her homeland with a pronounced, billowing waistline that emphasizes gyrating hip movement.

For some **onlookers,** she became the center of attention **for** both men and women. There was one gentleman bystander who locked eyes on her. His eyes followed her every alluring movement. When the song ended, and Fiona left the floor the wanting onlooker met her.

"Did you get that body at **McDonald's**?" The admirer asked.

"*Excusez-moi.*" Fiona leaned in to hear clearer.

"Ooo-la-la. A Frenchie. I said . . ." he spoke slower as if that would make his pitch more understandable ". . . did you get that body at **McDonald's**? Because 'I'm **lovin'** it.'" He earnestly stated. "Care to join me at my table?" **He invited.**

"*Non merci.*" She responded with a polite smile as she stepped aside and proceeded to her seat.

The **persistent** man followed **her escorted by Jaheim and his lyrics** to "Ain't Leavin' without You." ♪ *Hey girl how you doin'? I never seen nothing like you-like you. With a body, that shape, it's your claim to fame. And girl, I ain't leavin' without you.* ♪

Reaching the table, Fiona turned to **face** her pursuer. Instead of sitting next to Earl, she stood behind him in his chair. The pursuer brazened with swagger, he looked at Earl who was nursing a flute of champagne, and then he raised his gaze to Fiona.

"Are you sure?" The pursuer asked.

"I'm positive," Fiona assured him as she placed her hands on Earl's shoulders, and then slid them down the lapels of his suit jacket, over his broad chest.

The pursuer gave a side-eye glance, conceded with shrugged shoulders, and walked away.

֍֎֍֎֍

At Earl's home, the couple stood in the foyer right beneath the crystal chandelier. It was as if it was a scene of the prince and princess returning from the grand ball. He was dashing in his tuxedo. Fiona caught a subtle whiff of his *HiM* by *Honae Mori* cologne. It was her favorite scent on him, and she craved the smell to be infused on her bed sheets. Earl's eyes were transfixed on her freshly gloss coated, distinctly plump lips. He had a genuine fear of becoming possessed if ever caressing those lips with his.

They both were feeling the magic of the night, but neither would outwardly admit it. Awkwardly, neither of them could determine how seemingly platonic friends should end such an enchanted evening. It was Fiona who made the call.

"I'm so proud of you." She then kissed him on the cheek, deliberately as always to avoid direct lip contact with her good friend. Fiona coyly allowed the corner of her mouth to edge the corner of his. "*Bonne Nuit*," she bade, and then off she went to her preserved bedroom. She enjoyed the climb of the stairwell, catching a whiff of the Midsummer's Night Yankee Candle and the lingering scent of the patchouli soap coming from Earl's room.

Though they lay in adjacent rooms, their wondering thoughts were side by side. Those thoughts were musically laden. Fiona chose from her mobile phone's playlist, Chrisette Michele's "*A Couple of Forevers.*"

♪ *I see it clear, my heart is here*
We got each other and let's take it from there
And if I could I'd love you a forever end time

What we've been through, no one else knows
'Cause all that matters is how far this goes
And it will go until it starts again ♫

Earl went old school with the song he envisioned playing as Fiona walked in on at their wedding: Four Top's *"I believe in you and me."*

♫ *I believe in you and me*
I believe that we will be
In love eternally
As far as I can see
You will always be the one for me
Oh yes you will ♫

Sunday morning sunlight greeted Earl through the blinds of his bedroom windows and terrace doors. On exiting, he found that his overnight guest had gone. A voice message was left on the security alarm keypad. "Thank you for a wonderful night. Talk to you soon. Love you, babe"

Though he would never admit it out loud and before God, his heart felt a pang after hearing the message. Earl knew that he would not likely hear from Fiona again until she was back in town. Knowing she isn't one to call just to chitchat **or to check how he's doing. Neither does he** feel that he can call upon her because she's so busy with her work and the many others who pinch and pull on her time and attention. **He also knows that true friends can go long periods without speaking** – like they do and never question the friendship. That was his reasoning for keeping a guarded heart. The other stems from a heartbreaking memory.

"The thing about love is; just because you find it doesn't mean you can have it."

FLASHBACK

Earl's emotional intelligence, or the awareness of emotions and the emotions of those around him, helped enhance any interaction — especially when it comes to listening. That helped him become a confidant to Fiona. She felt comfortable telling him some things she may not be willing to tell her closest female friend. That automatically put Earl in the friend zone as far as Fiona was concerned. She consciously considered Earl as being soft as a man, because she was able to speak openly and freely with him.

Earl, on the other hand, felt that the closeness that he thought they shared meant that they were soulmates. They shared common interests and views – trust and confidence. He saw the potential in Fiona that she would be one day the accomplished person that she dreamt and spoke of being. He wanted to be there along with her side and to support her. The romantic in him romanticized their friendship and in his head and heart put them on a path of happily ever after.

It was one fateful afternoon that Earl decided to drop by and surprise Fiona with her favorite West African stew made with rice, chili peppers, and meat; called Jollof rice. Just as he arrived, he recognized his childhood friend Deshaun leaving out of Fiona's front door. Fiona could be seen struggling to close her robe. Earl waited until his friend drove away to give Fiona time to get decent. When she came to the answer the door and the bell; Fiona was still a little flushed and disheveled.

"Oh, I wish you would 'ave called. I was just about to jump into the shower." She explained.

"Then it wouldn't have been much of a surprise would it?"

"Oui."

Before they sat to share the African dish, Earl excused himself to wash his hands in the bathroom. While drying his hands on a hanging towel, he noticed in the open trash can what appeared to be a freshly discarded condom. A breath became held in his chest. A heartbeat skipped and paused. Angry tears flushed his eyelids. A yell was caught in his throat. His emotional intelligence left him dumbfounded. After regaining his composure, he returned to Fiona at the kitchenette table. He ate the food that had no flavor to him, and he never mentioned what he saw.

Four – Bedside, Holy Greens, and New Breath

"God allows things to happen to you, to work on your heart." –
Bishop Bronner

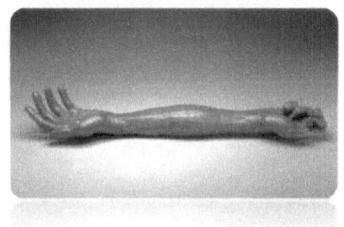

It was a comfortable 63 degrees with a partly sunny sky. Deshaun stole from the house early on Sunday morning to be among the first to tee off at Southeast Atlanta's Brown's Mill Golf Course. This was his religious sanctuary to lift his spirits and more importantly to help him relieve the stresses of his life. He pulled out a flask filled with Hennessy VS Cognac. Smirking as he took a swig of what he called his first communion at the Holy Greens. The humor of his church mocking was quickly lost in the moment when he heard in the back of his head, the voice of his sanctimonious wife scolding him.

"Chu going to get enough, of playing with God," chided his *Puerto Rican wife.*

"Nobody's playing."

"When is chu going to come back to church with me and Bradley?"

"When I fix me."

"Chu cannot fix chu. Only God and his Word can do that..."

This was a regular debate heard in the Howard house. Having not grown-up attending church Deshaun didn't have much respect for the religious institution. The respect that he did possess was enough to not be a hypocrite in attendance, being a nonbeliever. Despite his conviction and absence from the pews, Vera made sure Deshaun's presence was represented every other week by writing a **personal** check giving a tenth of his earnings as their tithes and offerings. Deshaun saw tithing to New Breath Baptist Church as one of the financial stressors in his life.

Of the four categorized stressors, insecurity, demanding routine, interpersonal conflicts, and traumatic events, Deshaun was affected by three. He swallowed hard after another mouthful of **liquor**. Ashamed to think of it as such, it was the traumatic event of the birth of his son that was his first pull back **into** the barrel. Complications began during the first trimester of the pregnancy. Vera had to stop her studies at Clark Atlanta University, and **she** inevitably dropped out of school during her senior year. The **pregnancy** complications carried through to the delivery where she experienced massive hemorrhaging, resulting in a maternal disability of severe anemia. The medical bills were double those of what normal childbirth would have been and neither **Deshaun nor Vera** had health insurance.

With Vera's moderate to severe anemia suffered from fatigue and lack of energy which dramatically reduced her productivity and quality of life. With also a slight case of post-partum depression, she was placed on Social Security Disability and a regimen of prescription medication. After a series of counseling sessions, it was revealed that Vera blamed Deshaun for all of her ill fates.

Vera's mother Maria Diaz came to live with the couple to help out and has remained. Maria's been with them from their one-bedroom apartment to their single-family home.

With the less-than congenial home life, Deshaun dedicated more of his time and attention to his work despite the relentless routine ninety-minute driving commute and long days. While it helped minimize face time and confrontations with Vera and the extended family, he seldom saw his teenage son. Deshaun chalked it up to the sacrifice of being a good provider for his family. Providing and enjoying the benefits of his labor was a struggle.

Even with promotions and cost of living increases that Deshaun received over the years, he found himself living from paycheck to paycheck and sometimes beyond. At one point Deshaun became caught up in the Payday loan cycle.

His contribution to filling the payment gap was with regular $50 tee times and $100 plus lap dances from his favorite stripper named Dreame at Magic City Adult Night Club. It maintained a healthy opinion of himself, as being a Lothario. This would not be his self-descriptive word; he would have used a more common term of a playboy. With his frequent visits to the world-famous Atlanta club, Deshaun was nicknamed "The Mayor of the City." While the Magic City's budget was balanced, The Mayor's was far from it.

Deshaun took a third unholy communion swig from his silver flask before he phoned Dreame. She did not answer. He then dialed his friend who has always been there for him.

"What 'sup EG?"

♫ *Easy like Sunday morning.* ♫ Earl sang. "What are you doing up so early on a Sunday? Did Vera finally get you to go to church with her?"

"Something like that. I'm at the Holy Greens."

"Where?"

"The golf course."

"You're so stupid." The two men **erupted** into a haughty laugh. "And here I thought Vera got you in a pew."

"*Mane*, you know how I feel about that church. When I did go; they always begging for money . . . got they hands out trying to get in my ass pocket. And Vera's like; bend over and give it to them and they don't **even** use any grease." Deshaun drew more laughter from Earl.

The effect of the alcohol was **relaxing the inhibition and** loosening Deshaun's tongue. "And how you going to be a bishop with a name like Bishop Freddie Proffitt?"

"De', the man can't help what his family name is."

"I mean come on now. You said yourself that's why you don't go to church. **Hey -did** you ever watch that YouTube video 'If I were the devil' by that old dude?"

"You mean Paul Harvey; no not yet."

"You need to check that shit out. Shit is happenin' just like he said. You smart for not giving your money away to these church people."

"No De', I believe in giving back. It just depends on how the giving is being handled. I support some causes and charities that have outreach ministries that make its way actually in the community. Yes, I've heard stories from people who've gone to these mega-churches for help with their utility cutoff notices and late rent due and have been turned away. Or, the administration of the church had the people jumping through more hoops than a Wall Street bank."

"You right EG, you know you right."

Earl had an opposing opinionated view of prosperity mega-churches in the black community. He felt that the preaching preyed on, the guilt of the middle class and upper income attending blacks who were first or second-generation college graduates like himself and Deshaun; who were likely the richest persons in their family line. For those like them, it was difficult to be happy with their riches when they have families living in poverty or always needed financial assistance.

With prosperity preaching Earl would hear, "one can feel comfortable knowing that they have money because their belief is stronger than others and because they are more giving than others therefore deserving to be rewarded. So it is not greedy when the pastor drives a Roll Royce instead of a Cadillac – flying in a private jet instead of in coach or business class. It's a testament to a faithful, guilt-ridden congregation."

"So how was the dinner?" Deshaun asked.

"It was nice. Fiona went with me."

"*Mane*, when are you going to *tap* that, if you haven't already?"

A long-forgotten memory began to resurface.

"*Nah* De', we're not like that."

"*Whatchu* waiting for?" Deshaun chided. "Someone is going to swoop that ass up and you're going to wonder what happened," Deshaun stated in earnest, as he was one of those who had the pleasure to be sexually intimate with Fiona. Since he's overcommitted with his marriage and side-chick relationship with Dreame, he covets Earl's wasted opportunities.

"That's a chance I'm going to have to take."

"So you do want to *tap that ass*?"

"She's a *wifey* candidate."

"Why marry her? The way you two hang, it's obvious that she likes you. She's probably just waiting for you to ask. You know them ball players she has been dating got between them Snicker thighs of hers and they ain't put a ring on it."

Earl took a millisecond pause before answering his friend. The truth of the matter was he did have regrets about the way he had approached the relationship with Fiona. He was torn between not waiting long enough and what could be considered waiting too long. He debated whether he would take Deshaun into his confidence and reveal how he once felt about Fiona. He knew that he wanted a long-term relationship with her versus temporal ejaculatory moments of pleasure. Not too many men would understand his position, so he decided to keep it to himself. Earl would also have to point out that his friend wasn't the best person to be giving relationship advice knowing that Deshaun took his marital problems to his exotic dancer - counselor.

Like his friend, Earl didn't subscribe to **any** organized religion, he considered himself ecumenical. That is a Gnostic. The Grey family went to a non-denominational Christian church. Like a growing number of those asked today, Earl considered himself more of a spiritual follower. He was an interfaith believer. He found that many churchgoers, especially those attending mega-churches misappropriate their faiths toward the person standing in the pulpit. To him, being spiritual **meant possessing a close relationship with** God.

He rationalized.

On most Sunday mornings, Earl was in attendance at Bedside Baptist, flipping through television channels to listen to whomever or whatever message caught his ear and seemed relevant to him. He watched as long as the televangelist was teaching how one can become a better person or if the message was focused on the common good of mankind.

That particular Sunday, Earl's channel surfing landed him on the Word of Faith program with Bronner teaching. "Never be afraid to correct what you've done wrong. It's always the right time to do right! There is no shame in getting right, the shame is in doing wrong. St. John Chrysostom put it this way, *'Be ashamed when you sin, not when you repent.'* Today is as good as any to right a wrong in your life. You don't have to wait till Sunday! Let the restoration begin!" **The bishop spoke.**

ৡৡৡৡ

At New Breath Baptist Church, the man at the podium spoke to the **after service was over** - stay behind members to attend a financial seminar.

"Christians should boldly ask God for new cars, a bigger house, and nice clothes . . . **Wealth** is a sign of God's favor. Riches and material goods are signs of a right relationship with God. We're going to show you how to get wealth and how to use it for the building of his kingdom," the venture capitalist **at the podium** proclaimed to the small **number of** congregates.

Vera heard divine words and the opportunity for redemption for a more than a decade-old transgression. "Finally," she thought to herself; "a chance to pay for my **sins**." For years she had been living with the guilt of keeping the money from the couple at the **abortion** clinic and spending it lavishly on herself. In the dark, she condemned herself and felt God had cursed her with the issue of blood. Now the light of God's forgiveness was shining on her, as she believed.

By the end of the presentation, Vera Howard was signing a personal check for five thousand dollars to a venture to support an inner-city community center for pregnant teens. Along with the **financial** support of the cause of unwed mothers, came a promised return of twenty percent on the investment. As soon as the return on the **venture** check would be in her hands, Vera envisioned redemption from a past transgression and a chance to show her husband that she can contribute moneywise to the household.

"Religion is following man's rules and traditions or grasping at superstitions."

Five – It's a Family Affair

"You can't pick your family you're born to, but you can pick the family you go through your life with." – Mina

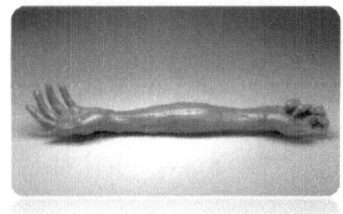

Adrian stood before the full-length mirror in his bedroom, admiring the reflection of himself. He was modeling his latest online purchase of Under Armour brand training gear. First on, were a pair of compression shorts; ultra-tight, second-skin fit delivering a locked-in feel that is supposed to keep his muscles fresh. To test the four-way stretch fabric, he did a few deep knee bends. Satisfied with the chafe-free movement, he grabbed his cell phone and took a selfie. Pleased with the "man in the mirror" pose, he sent it to Earl for his opinion. He waited a complete two minutes for a response while peering out the window of his midtown Atlanta, Atlantic Station loft. No response.

Miffed that Earl had not answered his text, Adrian decided to finish dressing for work. With a fastidious grooming routine he needed quite a bit of time; because he grooms and buffs his head and body, which he drapes in fashionable clothing. The term metrosexual was easily applied to Adrian as he had discretionary income to stay up to date with the latest hairstyles, the newest threads, and the right shaped shoes. He confused some guys when it came to his sexuality;

making these same guys jealous of his success with the ladies — for many metrosexuals, to interact with women is to flirt; impress the women who enjoy their company with the details that make the man.

Fully dressed and ready to embark upon the world, Adrian takes a last approving gaze at himself. It evokes a flashback to a darker beginning. It was the beginning of his grooming lifestyle that includes an idiosyncrasy of never wearing the same pair of underwear twice.

It was his first year in public school at six years of age. Raised by his mother and Busia, Adrian never had a man's influence in his life. Never shown how to urinate standing to hit the center of a Cheerio; he went into the school's boy's restroom unarmed and untrained. He saw a hanging wall urinal for the first time. His young mind could not process why the other boys faced the urinal standing to relieve their bladders.

Knowing the only way he knew how Adrian climbed on the porcelain fixture as best as he could to sit in an attempt to "take a leak." Amidst the laughter from his classmates and trying to hang on for his dear young life; Adrian lost his focus, and aim and he peed onto his clothes including his Thundercats' underpants. His teacher didn't take pity on him. By not bothering to call home to ask his grandmother to bring him a change of clothes, she had him sit in the back of the classroom for the rest of the day in his wet clothes.

"Never again," he said to the man in the mirror.

❧❧❧❧

The good thing about being raised by a woman, it gained Adrian a sensitive and keen ear for the feminine plight. While waiting in the women's bathroom accompanied by his grandmother; if the stalls, walls, and couch could talk; Adrian could hear them. That time spent listening to women's most intimate concerns was a contribution to his undiagnosed dissociative identity disorder. He heard voices. It also set him in his field of study at Morehouse College School of Medicine and the career path in gynecology. After graduating from college, he became a Physician Assistant at a prestigious OBGYN office in Atlanta. **The Midtown practice is** often frequented by local celebrities.

"Hello, Misses Wilson. I see you're here for a routine exam."

"Yes, Doctor Wiggins."

"Well then let's get started shall we and get you on your way. So do you have any concerns?"

Two voices replied.

First, Mrs. Wilson, "Doctor, have you ever seen or heard that skinny jeans can give you blood clots?" she asked.

Second, came, Mrs. Wilson's *vagina* voice: *"Psst, doctor. Doctor, I want to report an attempted murder. She's trying to suffocate me. I'm talking death by asphyxiation. Ever since she could squeeze into a pair of skinny jeans, that's all she wears all day, every day. And she knows what her mother told her when she was a girl - that - some things need to breathe. She* **meant** *me. Speaking of breathing; when she* **farts** *in* **those** *tight ass pants, you know that bubble is not going anywhere. Guess who suffers? You got it. And you know if I get sick, it ain't going to be pretty. So I'm begging you to talk to her, pulease."*

"Misses Wilson, **there was a summary of a study that** purported to **show that wearing skinny jeans can cause muscle and nerve damage by cutting off blood flow. You wouldn't want that would** you, **not with these** nice-looking calves **here?** Have you **been** working out?"

"Why, thank you, doctor. I did join a Zumba class."

"Well, it's paying off. Have you thought of wearing culottes **or some loose-fitting capris to show off** these legs?"

Vagina voice: "Thank you."

A whistle notification sounded, letting Adrian know that a text had come to his cellphone. He was hoping that it was Earl with a compliment on the selfie he had sent him earlier. It was not. Instead, it was a text from his younger stepsister Katelin Mason. He could see from the dating history that the last received text from her was nearly a year ago. It was the birth time of her third child, at Katelin's age of twenty-five. Then the text was to inform him that he was going to be an uncle again and to ask for money to be sent for her to purchase a phone card. After wiring the money, a thank you phone call from her never came, just another text, "ThanQ."

Katelin Text: "Hey big brother. How's it going in Atlanta? Have you met NeNe from *Real Housewives of Atlanta*?"

Adrian Text: "No I haven't."

Adrian shook his head in amazement at the disbelief of the people outside of Atlanta thinking that the population of the city consists of just those viewed on the reality television shows. If it wasn't for HIPAA (Health Insurance Portability and Accountability Act), the federal law that protects personal medical information; he could tell his little sister that he had indeed been between the legs of one or two of the *Real Housewives of Atlanta* and a few of the cast members from the *Love & Hip Hop: Atlanta* reality shows.

Katelin's employment and relationship history had been working at a minimum wage job at a hair salon, and dating a different guy who was a smooth talker and unemployed. She had been evicted from every apartment she had ever lived because she could not maintain paying the rent. She would text Adrian to borrow money; always running out of gas for her car or needing something for the kids. She tried to live off her student loan checks from pop-up vocational colleges. They were never enough to pay for the useless stuff for the deadbeat *baby daddies* and the things needed for her and the children.

Regardless of the painful childhood memory that Adrian's mother gave him up and chose a life with Katelin and Katelin's father; he felt a loyalty kinship toward his half-sister. So he would always answer her text request by sending her above and beyond the amount of money she asked for. In return, she would send an updated photo attached text of his nieces and nephew.

Katelin Text: "I need $1,000 by tmo 2 pay off sum old bills in order 2 get nto public housing that I've been onna waiting list for, for 2 years."

Six - A House is Not a Home.

"I realize, in its best disguise, a pretty house is not a home."
Somebody's Somebody lyric from Prince

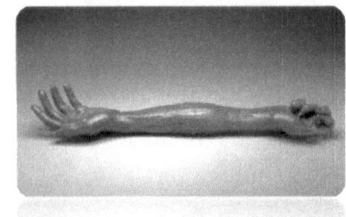

A midday popup thunderstorm set the mood for a lazy afternoon on the Westside of Atlanta. The usual Collier Heights Apartment sounds of children playing and mothers yelling are replaced by the boom of thunder. The rhythm of heavy raindrops played on the box fan wedged in the window. The scent of the fresh rain showers seeped into the bedroom window, mixing with the musky smell of incense, body sweat, and sex.

Deshaun stroked Dreame's bare behind who lay prone and naked atop the bed covers. He appreciated the smooth, muscle-toned hillocks of his girlfriend. His breathing returned to shallow. His body relaxed with the residual tingling of the fleeting orgasmic spasm. The chorus of "Love You Down" by Ready for the World played on the radio. The song and being in familiar surroundings as a kid made Deshaun homesick.

The Collier Heights Apartments as they were, reminded him of the conditions of "the Brands" the last time he was home in Odelot, Ohio. It was when he traveled home to bury his mother. Like the Collier Heights, the Brand Whitlock homes were considered a fairly good place to live for the rent but fell into decay and disrepair that worsened during the 1980s drug epidemic. Still, Deshaun's mother didn't want to move. She had lived there all of her life; in fact, she was the third generation in her family born and raised in the project homes.

Deshaun climbed out of bed and stood to look out the window at the pouring rain. There was an eerie quiet beyond the glass. Standing amid the rows of mostly empty brick buildings, their windows covered by plywood, he was witnessing what must have been the final days of Brand Whitlock Homes, where he was raised. Tattered curtains and broken blinds hung in a few windows. A potted plant was visible in a few still-occupied units in the building across a dirt field. Several doors sat wide open to invite a breeze. The Brands have since been demolished, but not before taking the life of Deshaun's mother. The news broadcast that ran for weeks on the local news replayed in his mind.

"The shooter fired at least six rounds – one of which pierced through a wood panel used to hold an air conditioning unit. The stray bullet went into an apartment, fatally wounding a woman. A teenager was wounded in the drive-by shooting early Tuesday morning, and a man was grazed by a stray bullet while inside his apartment. The shooting happened at the Brand Whitlock Homes in the central city of Odelot on the corner of Belmont and Nebraska Avenue."

Despite the long since bitter memories of project living, Deshaun felt more at home in Dreame's one-bedroom apartment than he did being in his suburban, 2,948 square foot single-family home with four bedrooms and 2.5 bathrooms. From the outside looking in - the Collier buildings looked dilapidated. Though on the inside, Dreame kept a very nice rent-to-own furnished apartment.

Deshaun often asked Dreame why wouldn't she move and he heard very familiar reasoning. "My grandmother stays next door and she doesn't want to move. Her friends still live here. The MARTA public transit bus comes up in here and picks her up right out front to take her to the doctors and wherever else she needs to go. Plus, our family is buried in the Lincoln Cemetery right over there." He understood her committed sense of family and community.

Deshaun wished he could feel that way once again. To him, his home was more of a dysfunctional boarding house with his wife, teenage son, mother-in-law, and brother-in-law living under his roof. He only knew his neighbors to wave at them.

He looked back from the window at Dreame who was sleeping soundly. A conviction of shame consumed him. It was not because he was having an affair with her; but for one he didn't know her full legal name - and two, he had no idea of any of her life's aspirations or her dreams.

❧❦❧❦❧

♪ ... *But a chair is not a house and a house is not a home. When there's no one there to hold you tight. And no* **one's** *there you can kiss goodnight ...♪* Luther Vandross melodically crooned through Earl's bedroom **Bose Wave System**.

The **rain** had not reached the east side of Atlanta, to "Decatur, where it's greater." The dark clouds were announcing the shower's **soon** arrival. In his bedroom, Earl sat in his Eames Lounge and Ottoman with both of the French doors open to his **upper** terrace. He could hear a family of birds chirping that were nesting above one of the **balcony's** columns. His view **of** the looming storm clouds was a carryover of the stormy night before.

After multiple exchanges of emails and phone conversations, Earl extended a dinner invitation to the online match found for him on Zoosk.com. He cooked mesquite maple steaks and vegetables with a side of new potatoes, with his choice of a Rex-Goliath Pinot Noir from his built-in wine cooler. The conversation over dinner continued as pleasantly **as they had been** *about their likes, dislikes, and common likes. Until . . .*

"Well Mister Earl Grey, I must say that I'm impressed. You're a man who cooked a fantastic meal. You have a beautiful home. By the way, in your den, I noticed the framed magazine covers on your wall. You didn't mention that you were a best-selling author. You're quite the Renaissance Man," she complimented.

"I'm not one to brag or boast."

"I actually have your book."

*"**Have** you read it?"*

"Honestly? I skimmed it. But what I read, I liked what you had to say. Anyway, look at you. You've got it going on."

"Thank you."

*"So why **is** a good catch like you not married?"*

"I don't know about me being 'a good catch.'"

"And you're modest."

*Modest is the word that best **describes** Earl Grey. After working several years as a highly successful advertising executive, he left **L.C. Arts & Advertising** as one of the top creative directors in the industry. He created, pitched, and sold a repeatable branding program to national retailers which made him a modest millionaire **from residuals**. Not even his closest friends were fully aware of his seven-figure net worth. He wrote a best-selling career **guidebook**, "A Better You Means a Better We."*

*He **is** gifted with the ability to listen to people and to identify their God-given strengths, potential, and natural talents. In doing so, he **travels** the country pitching to major corporations on the topics of executive leadership and building personal and professional **networks**. His speaking fee **was** fifteen thousand dollars, plus expenses per engagement.*

"May I ask you a personal question?" She asked.

"Sure."

"Tell me about your last relationship; I mean why it didn't work out." She assumed it didn't work or they wouldn't have met on a dating website.

"Seriously?" Earl asked with genuine skepticism. He thought that past relationships fell into the "don't ask don't tell" category.

"You said 'sure,' that I could ask."

*Standing from the **formal** dining room table, **Earl** walked over and extended his hand. He then escorted his internet date to his fully stocked wet bar. She took a seat on one of the leather bar stools, while he took his **position** behind the bar. After learning her drink preference, he mixed her a screwdriver with Grey Goose Le Melon. For himself, he poured a shot of Dalwhinnie 15 Scotch Whiskey. All the while, he's thinking about what level of detail of his past he would share.*

"Well, I actually dated twins." Earl opened with.

"Ooooooookay." A thread arched eyebrow raised over one eye, as she became intrigued.

"Their names were Needy and Greedy."

"Come on," she followed with a chuckle.

"I'm serious."

"Alright, go on."

*"I met Needy first while living in the West End area of Atlanta after graduating from college. I was in line at a corner store when I noticed this very pretty girl a few people ahead. She had some unnatural features that made her look exotic – light complexion with sandy-colored hair and **bubblegum pink** lips. **To** top it all off, she had a*

diamond stud piercing in the crease of her nose. Yes, I fell in love with her looks at first. But she also had this quiet grace. She wasn't your typical around the way girl from the hood. I nicknamed her Ghetto Rose.

"You say that I'm a good catch now, back then I was what most would consider a nerd. I had no game, certainly no swagger. But I mustered the courage to approach her. She looked me up and down and said; 'you's a preppy.' Her condescending tone let me know that it wasn't a compliment. Still, I persuaded her to go out with me.

"I didn't have a car yet. I was riding MARTA. For our first date, I took her to Centennial Park for an afternoon picnic, and then we hung out at the CNN Center. On our next date, we went to the Hammonds House Museum. She had never been inside the museum, even though she lived right around the corner from it. From there, things between us kind of cooled off.

"When I would call her she was always too busy to go out. Often, my phone calls would go unanswered. Her mother would talk to me and ask that I keep trying to make it work with her daughter. Her mother liked me. And when I would hear from Needy, it was always that she would need to get her hair and nails done as a condition if we were to go on a date. Sometimes she would ask if I would buy her an outfit to wear from the West End Mall. This was fine with me; I wanted her to look nice. Then the frequency of her calling me became every two weeks when I got paid.

"The first time that I told her 'no' because I had bills of my own; she caught an attitude. She then confessed; 'I like a guy with a little thug in him' so we stopped seeing one another because I was not that guy. The next time I laid eyes on her after the breakup was much like the first time. We were in line at the corner store. She bought a pickle from the large jar on the counter and a Fanta grape pop. When she turned around I saw that she was glowing prettier than ever before. She was radiant because she was a few months pregnant. Oh, it wasn't mine. I never had the pleasure.

"We hugged and I congratulated her on the pregnancy. 'I guess you found your thug,' I offered. 'Yeah, well his ass went and got some other girl pregnant,' was Ghetto Rose's response. I didn't know what to think or to say. I was jealous. I was mad and I felt sorry for her. We were cool for a couple of months after that. I stepped right back in helping out financially until the thug daddy came back **into** the picture. And that was that." Earl concluded.

"I'm not sure who was the **needier** one from that story," stated the **female** dinner guest before taking a **sip** of her drink.

"Yeah, I suppose."

"So tell me about her twin?"

"Who?"

"Greedy."

"Oh yeah, right. Would you like for me to refresh your drink?"

"Please." After refreshing their drinks, Earl suggested they move to his sitting room. He turned down the volume on his **home theatre system** which was streaming Pandora to his Luther Vandross Radio selections.

"So, about Greedy; though they were twins, you couldn't tell it from looking at them. Greedy had a polished appearance all the time. From the first day we met at a happy hour mixer, she never had a bad hair day. Unlike Needy, Greedy had a good-paying job, drove a Lexus, and was buying a three-bedroom home. When it came to us dating; she would often flip the script on me. She would choose the restaurant and pay the check. She wouldn't even let me leave the tip. As far as entertainment events; always front row, floor seats.

"Though it was a refreshing change, I was uncomfortable with the role reversal. At this time, I was doing well career-wise. I didn't have a house, but I had a nice apartment. Things became pretty serious between us and we decided to live together. I gave up my apartment. That's when I got a **peek** behind the velvet curtains.

"Let me **back up**. Here I was thinking that I met someone on equal *financial* footing as me. She may have been pulling in more money than I was at the time. She was a good-looking professional woman who could talk **about** current events and sports. Before moving in, we had gone on a cruise to the Bahamas and we flew to St. Louis for her family reunion. Appearance-wise, we looked like the perfect couple. **Her people** were talking about marriage.

"Okay, so now I'm moved in and naturally I began pitching in on the household bills. I was raised that a man is supposed to be the provider. As the provider, I wanted to know exactly what it was I providing for. So I asked Greedy for a full disclosure of the household expenses. What also brought this on was that Greedy had started asking me to pitch in more and more towards the **household expenses**. I was curious as to why when I knew I hadn't contributed more to the increase **in** utilities and what have you. It was she that had the cable premium package so that she could keep up with Bravo's "The Real Housewives" of six different cities.

"Greedy didn't have a budget plan per se."

"Per say?" **She questioned.**

"What, you never met a man who's **witty** and urbane?" Earl questioned **in return**.

"Not one who openly admitted it. I'm sorry, go ahead, finish."

"Thank you. Greedy paid the bills on an on-demand basis. Past due and disconnection notices were the demand. When I got her to sit down with me and prepare a budget and expense document it was all revealed. This pseudo-successful woman was all a front. She was living from paycheck to paycheck though she did indeed earn more than me. Greedy brought home better than six figures, but she had a sixteen-hundred-dollar house note, six hundred **dollars a month** car *payment and the rest* **went toward credit cards** *to keep up the appearances of a lavish lifestyle. She was living beyond her means.*

"When I **challenged** *her spending habits and to get her to make concessions; her response was 'well you're here aren't you.' Though not as much, I had my debt to pay down. This led to a discussion about our long-term goals. She didn't want to downsize the house because she wanted to have a couple of kids. She also had planned on moving her mother in with her. Both the idea of kids and the mother moving in were news to me. But I didn't dismiss the idea. But I told her that no matter the case, – her spending habits and lifestyle would need to change.*

'Greedy lived off of her credit cards when her salary didn't cover her expenses and she didn't have a hundred dollars saved in the bank. She continued her weekly hair salon, manicure-pedicure appointments, and buying high-end purses and shoes. When we would go out, she had to eat at the fanciest restaurants. Her justification was thrown in my face as; 'you want me to look good for you don't you. You didn't complain when I looked like this when you met me.' And this was a clincher; **she would say** *'Oh these shoes - they were on sale.'*

"From that point, we couldn't seem to agree on many things. One day when I came home from work, my things were packed in boxes and were waiting for me at the door. I moved **out and** *in with one of my boys until I could get my place. There you have it, my last dating experiences."*

"So you pretty much put women in two categories, needy or greedy."

"Not all."

"Wow. So why am I here?"

"Maybe to change my mind?"

"I'll have you **to** *know; I am* **the** *total package. I brought home two-hundred thousand last year, while you're out hustling books. I have a*

*luxury home with an alarm system, a nine-millimeter inside, and a guard dog. I don't need you to help me budget **or protect** my money. I pay people to do that for me. I am and can do well all by myself." She declared **the single woman's anthem**.*

*By the time she went through a litany of "I can do **this**, I have this and that and I don't need;" she also **threw** in quite a few personal shots at Earl's character and manhood.*

*"Are you sure you aren't **a closeted** gay? I need a real man, not a sissy. No woman will marry you with that attitude. Creeps like you will never get laid! If you didn't go after hoochies, then they wouldn't want your money. Step up and take a chance like a man! You're afraid of a strong woman! You need to **get over** being so negative toward women who might need help. You are so cynical. I bet you don't have more than a handful of friends, do you? If you refuse to have relationships with women, then you are admitting defeat. Guys like you are scary. You're just afraid of losing your male privileges. You're protecting your fragile male-**sensitive** ego. You're unstable. You have issues. You need therapy. At this rate, you're going to end up all alone." She decreed.*

"Sometimes you have to stand alone to prove that you can stand at all." Earl offered.

Seven - Comin' from Where I'm From.

"Everyone who comes with you can't go with you."

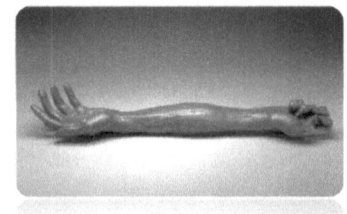

Eleven o'clock post meridian, Central Standard Time. Fiona laid wide awake in the king-sized bed at the Hyatt Grand Hotel in Chicago, Illinois. She was still teary-eyed and giddy; from the news she had received at dinner from her Executive Manager. "Fiona, you *have* now *been promoted to* a director and you will be making this amount of money starting next pay period." The manager announced as he showed her on his electronic tablet her new six-figure plus salary.

Unable to sleep because of the recent good news, Fiona sat up in the oversized bed and turned on the nightstand lamp. The lamp illuminated a hotel suite with a cozy corner sofa-sleeper in the living room space, a dining area, and a small kitchenette. The spacious suite was equivalent to the size of the single-story home that she grew up in with her parents and six brothers until she was eleven. During that time, Fiona never had a room or a bed to herself. She shared a girls' room and bed with aunts and live-in female housekeepers. In Cameroon, housekeepers or maids may be common and they are mostly from the rural areas with little education. They get paid about $50 a month along with the room and board.

With her mind drifting back to days in Africa; when an eleven-year-old girl had dreams of success and coming to America – *"terre d'accueil"* (land of welcome). Fiona, like many other Cameroonians, had the misconception that in America, money grew on trees, there was no need to work, Americans were passionate about everything, no suffering, no homeless, no diseases, no unpaved roads and it was close to Heaven. It was unlikely to Fiona that she would ever touch the soils of the United States of America because her family was relatively poor.

Relative poverty was a term used on the news to mean people who had less money than those living around them. Absolute poverty referred to a condition where a person does not have the minimum amount of income needed to meet the minimum requirements for one or more basic living needs over an extended period, including food, clean water, sanitation facilities, affordable health care, and education. But in African countries, people living in sub-Saharan Africa live in absolute poverty.

Living in relative poverty, Fiona realized; you don't have to be wealthy to be happy, as long as you have enough to live on. She was happy as a child, living in an overcrowded house. She slept in what was called the "girl's room;" this was the room where her aunts and maids also slept. There were two people per bed. The love of family was enough to live on.

The **emotional** restraint weakened. Tears began to stream down her face. A small release of joy and **giggles** escaped her lips. She had to talk to someone or she would have an **emotive** burst. Who **are** you *gonna* call? The question would prove difficult for Fiona to answer. She considered the **handful** of friends she had to call on.

Usually, people don't get a lot of training **in** evaluating character, so **they** choose people based on their outward appearance, and then **they** experience the inside of them. Fiona had a few boyfriends and a one-time fiancé who **was** able to start a relationship but couldn't finish it. They talked commitment and companionship but left her **once they got what they wanted or** when she needed them most.

Calling one of them would only have them coming not with open arms, but with the beggar's hands or a **wish** to get in bed with her.

She had a mentor whom she once respected. Though he was judgmental, he spoke the truth without love and had no room for grace or forgiveness. He called **Fiona** cajoling and that she dressed to persuade men to get what she wanted. Fiona was not sure how to take his criticism, because she often caught him eyeing her backside as she walked away.

Then there was Kendra, her housemate. She would be genuinely happy for Fiona, but for selfish reasons. Kendra had a problem with delaying gratification. She put wants before needs. **Stereotypically, she buys what she WANTS and begs for what she needs.** She **didn't** follow through on her commitments. **Financially** and emotionally **she's** irresponsible and **relied** on Fiona for stability. Learning of Fiona's promotion and raise would have her looking at it for her benefit.

After applying discernment, Fiona ruled out the handful of people she considered. There was only one other. He was her 6FF (sixth finger friend – **a friend that you call on, when the other handful can't or won't do**) as he called himself. He told Fiona she could call on him whenever she had no one else to count on.

*The last time that she called upon **her** 6FF for emotional support was when she was having a moment - when her grandmother had died. Just before receiving the sorrowful news from one of the family members that her grandmother had been caring for; the seemingly foretelling Diane Reeve's song "Better Days" aired on the radio. Fiona was quite shaken as tears in her eyes burned and she was blubbering into her phone.*

Once dialing his **cell phone** number, she heard the **Dave Brubeck** smooth jazz answer tone **rendition** of *"Take Five."* On the receiving end, the phone rang with the specially selected ringtone *"Still a Friend of Mine,"* performed by Incognito. **Earl** knew who was calling.

"*Parle moi*," Earl answered.

"*Bon soir Earl,* **como tale vu**?

"*Oh bonjour Fiona, ca va bien merci et toi*? He replied with the rehearsed French response.

"*Very* good *babe*. You've been practicing."

"Just a little."

"Were you asleep?" Fiona suddenly became aware that it was after midnight in his time zone.

"No. I was reviewing some notes. I'm going to be on a panel tomorrow at Emory University discussing creating a digital personal brand."

"Oh, then I should let you get back to work."

"No, no it's okay. I needed the break."

"You sure?"

"Yes. So what's up?"

"Well, I 'ave some good news."

"Do share."

Fiona commenced sharing the highlights of the dinner with her Executive Manager; the promotion, the accolades for her performance, and of course the salary increase. She went from a calm disclosure to an exciting ramble.

"This is my dream come true," she continued. "When I was much younger; I **always** knew that I wanted to be a **businesswoman**. I wanted to dress nice and run things like the woman I saw in the movie *Boomerang*. I think 'er name was Robin. Eddie Murphy was in the movie too."

"You mean, Robin Givens."

"Yes, that's 'er. I loved 'er in that movie. Did you see it and what did you think of 'er?"

"Yes I saw it. The funny thing is; it was *Maaaarcus'* character that made me want to go into advertising."

"Really?! Now that you say that, you do remind me of 'im."

"I hope in a good way."

"*Oui.*"

"So now your dream has come true."

"*Oui*, but it is both a blessing and a curse."

"How so?"

"I've shared with you the blessings' part, no? The curse that it brings is . . ." a cautious pause. "With the more money, my family back 'ome will think of me as rich. I already send them money. They will now expect even more. This is sometimes called the Black Tax."

"More money, more problems," Earl responded with the Notorious B.I.G. mantra. "The more money you make, the more problems you get. That's real. It comes with the territory."

"*Exactement.* Please don't think bad of me or my family. I want to 'elp my family. It's not the ones I am paying back for 'elping me come to America."

"Then who is it?"

"Please don't think badly of my family."

"Will you stop asking me that?"

"I'm sorry. It's, it's . . ."

"What?"

"I 'ave not gone 'ome to my 'omeland for some time, because of what 'appened the last time I was there. I traveled 'ome to stay for three weeks. I bought clothes and shoes and packed two bags. I 'ad some electronic gifts for my father and brothers. I stayed with a cousin because my parents 'ouse was too crowded. On that visit, my luggage was stolen from my cousin's 'ouse."

"What!?"

"Yes, all of my clothes and belongings for the trip 'ad been taken."

"*Sooooooo*, what did your cousin say happened?"

"She said she didn't know, but she did 'elp me look for them. Do you remember that time I called you and asked you to deposit some money into my bank account?"

Earl had recalled the incident from a few years ago. Fiona asked to borrow a couple of thousand dollars. She needed to renew her Certificate of Naturalization Citizenship and for travel costs to the American Embassy in Cameroon. She vowed to pay him back insisting on drafting a promissory note between them.

Fiona went on to tell the painful story of her last trip to the village where she lived in Yaoundé, the capital of Cameroon. Despite Earl's earlier request, she continued to beg him not to think badly of her family. She explained that some of the people there were materialistic. Defending her culture; materialism equated to status in Cameroon and that people living in America had it so easy.

Sentiment crept into her voice as she spoke of her people and began reminiscing about home. She was the only girl in a family of seven children. The memories were of times when she would beat boys racing on the unpaved roads. She enjoyed attending the Catholic school back home, where Sister Mary Anne recognized Fiona's eagerness to learn and winsome aptitude. After graduating from primary school, Fiona begged her parents to let her come to America to live with her aunt. They agreed.

There was what is called a Njangi sendoff party, where money was raised to send with her. Her father told her; "Don't forget where you come from."

In regard to maintaining her virtue; "My father took a good look at me. Then 'e sat me down on 'is lap and said something that I will never forget; 'e looked me straight in the eyes and said, *'Fiona, everything that God made valuable in the world is covered and 'ard to get to. Where do you find diamonds from Sierra Leone?'"* 'e asked.

"Deep down in the ground," I answered.

"' Yes," 'e said "covered and protected. One must work 'ard to get to them. Your body is such *a jeweled gift. You're far more precious than diamonds and you should keep covered too."*

There came a long pause in her storytelling allowing her thoughts to travel to when she arrived in America. She left Africa for America on her twelfth birthday to live with her elderly aunt who was a live-in Home Healthcare worker for a Jewish family in Bronxville, New York. The wealthy family had sponsored Fiona's aunt and her in getting their Green Cards. Fiona took a great interest in the health services her aunt provided to their host family.

In high school, she enrolled in a STEM program for advanced female students. The program focused on the academic disciplines of Science, Technology, Engineering, and Mathematics. She graduated from high school at sixteen; Class Valedictorian with a 4.0 GPA. She was always socially active and became President of the National Honor Society. After receiving over $100,000 in scholarships, she went to study at Spelman College in Atlanta.

Well into the early morning Fiona shared with Earl her *Coming to America* incidental accolades and blessings.

"Je ne sais pas ou le temps s'est enfui." Fiona eloquently spoke.

"Come again?" Earl asked.

"Funny 'ow time flies when you're 'aving fun. *Oui*" she translated the Janet Jackson lyric.

"You're right, look at the time."

"I'm sorry for keeping you up."

"That's what friends are for."

"There aren't many people in my life that whom I can share my intimate thoughts. Thank you for being someone who understands me."

"My pleasure *Mon Amie*. Good night, Fiona."

"*Oh je t'aime mon chéri.*"

Eight - With Money I'm Poor.

"Middle-class negroes have forgotten their roots and are untouched by the struggles of their underprivileged brothers." – Martin Luther King, Jr.

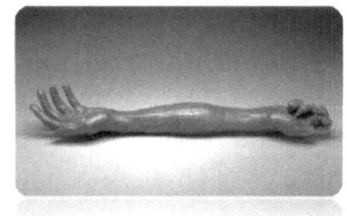

After a long day at work and an hour in traffic, Deshaun was glad to be home, parked in the driveway of his Glore Crossing Drive, in Mableton, Georgia. He looked forward to a glass of brandy and hopefully the peace of the evening. The lawn had not been cut. This meant a fight with his son Bradley about doing his chores to earn his allowance. It was at these times that he envied Earl the most for his carefree lifestyle. No responsibility for family and there being no one other than him in that big house of his.

Deshaun closed the front door of his house and was greeted by loud language coming from the family room. It was the all too familiar Spanglish being shouted. When Vera was angry, she often spoke it. From what he could make out, Eddie, Vera's brother was being blamed for stealing twenty dollars from his mother's purse. The money was his mother's set aside to play the lottery. Eddie wasn't there to defend himself.

There was another point of contention between the mother and daughter. Vera was late picking her mother up from the MARTA H.E. Holmes rail station. This wasn't a new argument for the two women. Maria Diaz worked as a **home care** worker for a family who lived north of Forsyth County, Georgia. She **had** to travel over an hour's ride to the furthest north rail station. From there she caught a bus to a park and ride to be picked up by the people for who she kept house.

"I be tired after cleaning house all day. *Den* I have to sit around at the bus station only makes it *worster*." The mother spews at her daughter.

"I said that I was sorry. I have things to do too you know." Vera spits back.

"You couldn't tell by the looks of *dis* place."

Vera **didn't** keep **the** house well despite her self-proclaimed stay-at-home *House Goddess* title. This **had** been a source of dispute between Deshaun, Vera, and their son as well. The bad habit of not picking up after himself **had** carried over to their teenager. Ironically, **Mama Diaz had** enabled the both of them by extending her housekeeping duties to their house. Household chores are Deshaun and Maria's commissary bond since she moved in with them when Bradley was born.

Bradley Howard had grown up to be somewhat of a selfish and spoiled teenager. Because of the complications of his birth, the special attention **he'd** received **had** negatively influenced his behavior. He **had** been coddled and cared for to the point that he **saw** whatever **was** given to him as an entitlement. Being of African American and Puerto Rican **blend**, Bradley **had** a handsome colorful appeal. He **used** his looks and **charisma** to get what he **wanted**, especially from females. His father **had** tried his best to raise him to be responsible, but his efforts **were** often thwarted by Vera. The person who **had** the most positive influence over him **was** his godfather, Earl Grey.

While Earl did not miss a birthday or a gift-giving occasion to bestow on his godson; it was never something lavishing. Bradley and Earl had the frequent heart to heart conversations. From those talks, Earl gained insights into what he felt Bradley needed and provides them – leaving his wants to others to give him.

"Where's Bradley?" Deshaun asked his wife as he poured himself a glass of Paul Masson brandy.

"Well hello and how are you too."

"Sorry. Hello honey" acknowledging his wife, then his mother-in-law "Mama Maria."

"He's over to the Anderson's for Bobby's birthday party."

"I said he couldn't go unless he cut the grass."

"Bobby is his best friend. How could he not go?"

"That's not the point . . ."

"Oh here we go again" Vera exclaimed.

❦❦❦❦❦

♫ *Happy birthday to you. Happy birthday dear Bobby. Happy birthday to you.* ♫

Family and friends stood around as they watched Bobby Anderson open his gifts and birthday cards. Among his gifts, he received the latest electronic gaming console, with an assortment of games to play. The birthday cards which were the most popular gifts he received were filled with gift cards to various stores. Hardly anyone gave cash anymore. Bradley excused himself to go into Anderson's half bath. From his back pocket, he pulled out the birthday card he intended to give his best friend. Removing the twenty-dollar bill he stole from his grandmother's purse, he shoved it in his pocket, then tore the card into small pieces and flushed them in the toilet.

৵৵৻৶৻৲

Eduardo "Eddie" Diaz de-boarded the Cobb County Transit bus that let him off right around the corner from the Howard's home. It had been a long money hustling day for him. In the morning he made his second visit for the week giving blood at a Plasma Donation Center. Forty-five dollars was placed on his issued debit card. Right afterward, Eddie purchased a couple of packs of Newport cigarettes and proceeded to sell them as *loosies* at the MARTA Five Points Station in downtown Atlanta. A single cigarette can go for fifty cents. The competition was steep where buses let outriders on their way to work at the central transit hub.

"Newport. Newport" is the callout. Young and old sellers, even wheelchair bound are a part of the street hustle.

This particular day was bad for business for Eddie. He was picked up by an undercover Atlanta police officer on a solicitation charge. The officer pointed out the posted sign sighting the City of Atlanta Code Section 43-1 ordinance. Because it was a misdemeanor offense, he was only given a citation and released on his recognizance without having to post bail. The cigarettes and cash were confiscated. With that on his mind, he had a long walk home and did not know what waited for him when he would get there.

৵৵৻৶৻৲

Sunday morning, Maria Diaz and Vera Howard sat in the pews eagerly awaiting the words of Bishop Proffitt. The men of the Howard household; Deshaun, Eddie, and Bradley stayed home. For his sermon of the day, the Bishop read an email that he received.

"There once was a man named George Thomas, a preacher in a small Texas town. One Sunday morning he came to the Church building carrying a rusty, bent, old bird cage, and set it by the pulpit. Eyebrows were raised and as if in response, the Preacher began to speak. . . .

"I was walking through town yesterday when I saw a young boy coming toward me swinging this bird cage. On the bottom of the cage were three little wild birds, shivering with cold and fright.

"I stopped the lad and asked, 'What do you have there, son?'

"Just some old birds,' came the reply.

"What are you going to do with them?' I asked.

"Take 'em home and have fun with 'em,' he answered. 'I'm gonna tease 'em and pull out their feathers to make 'em fight. I'm gonna have a **really** good time.'

"But you'll get tired of those birds sooner or later. What will you do then?'

"Oh, I got some cats," said the little boy. 'They like birds. I'll take 'em to them.'

"The preacher was silent for a moment. 'How much do you want for those birds, son?'

"Huh? Why, you don't want **these** birds, mister. They're just plain old field birds. They don't sing. They ain't even pretty!'

"How much?' the preacher asked again.

"The boy sized up the preacher as if he were crazy and said, 'ten dollars?'

"The preacher reached in his pocket and took out a ten-dollar bill. He placed it in the boy's hand. In a flash, the boy was gone. The preacher picked up the cage and gently carried it to the end of the alley where there was a tree and a grassy spot. Setting the cage down, he opened the door, and by softly tapping the bars persuaded the birds out, setting them free. Well, that explained the empty bird cage on the pulpit, and then the preacher began to tell this story:

"One day Satan and Jesus were having a conversation. Satan had just come from the Garden of Eden, and he was gloating and boasting. "Yes, sir, I just caught a world full of people down there. Set me a trap, used bait I knew they couldn't resist. Got 'em all!'

"What are you going to do with them?' Jesus asked.

"Satan replied, 'Oh, I'm gonna have fun! I'm gonna teach them how to marry and divorce each other, how to hate and abuse each other, how to drink and smoke and curse. I'm gonna teach them how to invent guns and bombs and kill each other. I'm really gonna have fun!'

"And what will you do when you are done with them?' Jesus asked.

"Oh, I'll kill 'em,' Satan glared proudly.

"How much do you want for them?' Jesus asked.

"Oh, you don't want those people. They ain't no good. Why you'll take them and they'll just hate you. They'll spit on you, curse you and kill you. You don't want those people!'

"How much?' He asked again.

"Satan looked at Jesus and sneered, 'All your blood, tears, and your life.'

"Jesus said, 'DONE!' Then He paid the price.

"The preacher picked up the cage and walked from the pulpit."

Bishop Proffitt said to the New Breath congregation; "I pray, for everyone who remembers this story when you leave the church. Tell it to those who you know didn't make it to service today. Remind them to thank God every day for their blessed life. Though they may not be rich, don't live in a mansion on the hill, and don't have the nicest of material things, but, they have a roof over their head, clothes on their back, food on their table, a family that loves them and lifelong friends to get them through. Say to them that they have a lot to be thankful for. Amen."

On the **drive** home, Vera both cried and prayed silently in thanks for her life and lifestyle. Afraid to look over to the woman in the passenger seat **of the Ford Escalade**, the woman who bore her life, Vera looked straight ahead. As the bishop foretold, a price had indeed been paid for her life to "NOT come to term."

Maria Diaz, a hot, sexy, and young *Boriqua* came to Atlanta, Georgia in search of a better life. As an undocumented alien, she found work as a housekeeper for a very wealthy Wellington family in **North Georgia.** That was not all that she thought she found. Naïve, misguided, and seduced by money, trinkets, and security, Maria became involved in an affair with her employer, Master Wellington. Once she became pregnant he called her a *puta* (a whore) in her language and she was given five thousand dollars to abort the baby and go away quietly. It was like a script out of a primetime soap opera.

She adhered to one out of the two bribery conditions. Supposedly, voluntarily quitting her job, she moved into an extended stay hotel and nine months later, Vera Diaz was born.

Unable to find sustainable work and with the bribery money exhausted, Maria quickly connected with the first man willing to have her and to accept a ready-made family. She and the new man had a child, Eduardo. The children were considered anchor babies because they were born on US soil. Unfortunately, the new man was also an undocumented worker and was caught up in a customs sweep at a construction worksite by the U.S. Immigration Customs and Enforcement (ICE) department and he was deported. He made no mention of Maria and the children to ICE.

Unable to financially support herself and the children; they had to move to the City of Refuge, a shelter for homeless families. There, Maria attempted to commit suicide. She was placed in Georgia

Regional Hospital in Atlanta for a month of mental observation. The children were placed in the custody of the childcare system. With the aid of antidepressant medication and therapy, Maria was released and returned to the shelter.

At the shelter, Maria befriended an above and beyond performing case worker who helped reunite her with her children. **Learning of Maria's background, she** also convinced Maria to reach out to the Wellington's **for assistance**.

Nine - Don't Compare. Compete. Complain.

Don't brag. Don't boast. Don't blow your own horn.

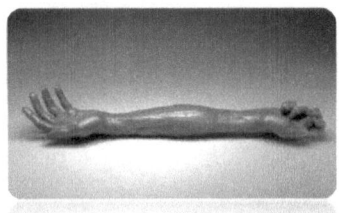

Earlene Grey **was** an attractive modern woman. At the age of fifty-seven, she **does not** have a single strand of gray hair on her head or **growing** anywhere else on her body. Her figure **is not** as shapely as she would like, but it **is** slim and enviously looked upon by other middle-aged women. She's not your dowdy AARP card-carrying woman. Any given day, Earlene might be wearing ripped jeans, and a hip, cool flowing top, sporting long hair with highlights and a Brazilian wax for only some to see.

While she still manages to turn **the** heads **of men** in the grocery store; Earlene pays them no mind. She knows that she is a catch. **The** Fifties is the perfect stage of life for women, as men are seeking them out for relationships. They are mature, working and for the most part, **they** are empty nesters. Women in their 50s have lived life and are a bit more reality-based **than** their younger counterparts. The best news is that their biological clock is done ticking, so no fear **or want** of more little ones!

There **is** one other factor that has kept Earlene a single woman. She doubts that any man can treat her better than her son, Earl. After buying her a house and a car for her; he either joins or sends her and a friend on a cruise trip every year. She has plans for her and Earl to one day travel to the Holy Land. While the common observer would see the care that Earl bestows upon his mother as being a good doting son, it comes from another motivation.

Since Earlene's husband Earl, Sr. died in the Persian Gulf War when Earl was nine, she has not been the same. Her husband and she were childhood sweethearts since the first-grade pigtail pulling, their high school prom until death did they part. Of the five stages of grief; denial, anger, bargaining, depression, and acceptance, Earlene never moved past denial. In her mind her husband did not die; he abandoned them and she had never forgiven him. Though it was not officially diagnosed, she suffered from a form of post-traumatic stress disorder.

At an early age, Earl Grey, Jr. became the man of the house and had been raised to be the provider man he has become. After taking on manhood responsibilities, there wasn't time for friends and playtime. Instead, he immersed himself in academics earning him the nickname "EGG-head" for being a nerd. His dutifulness to his studies afforded him enrollment in the collegiate Odelot EXCEL scholarship incentive program. Coupled with the GI Bill, Earl gained a fully paid college scholarship. He was blessed so abundantly that he even received a scholarship for being left-handed.

"Earl Grey, the principal of IT'S ME Inc., is a best-selling author, entrepreneur, and thought leader in brand strategy. His patented formula has impacted clients such as professional athletes, celebrities, and executives of Fortune 500 corporations. He lectures on insights from business and philanthropic tycoons who are having a positive influence on the world every day." Using her electronic tablet, Earlene read to her friend Judith the profile from an online magazine.

"That's my son." Earlene proudly announced.

Judith mustered a placid smile in response to her coworker and longtime friend from the Odelot Old Town Community Organization (O.O.T.C.O.) neighborhood in which they once lived. That was before

Earl moved Earlene ten miles and thirty minutes in travel time away from the inner city. Judith does not drive and gets around using public transportation. Also, she relies on family members to take her grocery shopping. To visit her Earlene, it would take her an hours ride

"I am so proud of that boy," Judith genuinely conveyed to her coworker at St. Have Mercy Medical Center. She has known Earl since his birth. That lifetime acquaintance with the family was why Earl includes her on the annual sea excursions with him and his mother. When he cannot vacation with them, he still sends the two of them.

Judith's three children and Earl were around the same age and attended school together. Her husband walked away from the family and started another. Her oldest son was on the streets, strung out on drugs. The middle son died in a suspected drug deal gone wrong. Her youngest child, a daughter, became pregnant at sixteen and left the house and married the father of the child. The daughter is now in an abusive relationship and does not come around to visit her mother. Painfully, Judith has had to come to terms with; *"if someone wants to be a part of her life, they'll make an effort to be in it."* Without her children in her life, Judith has vicariously been adopted into the Grey family.

Sitting across from the break room table, Judith listened to Earlene go on about the successes of her son and all the wonderful things she expects him to do and buy for her. Not once does Earlene consider Judith's feelings. It does not matter. Judith is content with her status in life and circumstances. Through it all, she had stood firm, stayed strong, and stayed focused. She's embraced the thought; "anything that I wasn't born with, I don't have to have."

Earlene, on the other hand, is not thankful and does not recognize that right across from her was someone more than happy with less.

Ten – Praying Grandmother.

"How many people you bless is how you measure success."

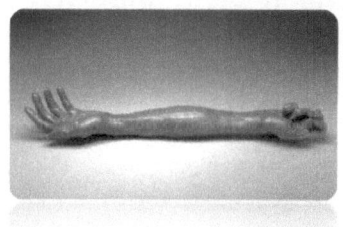

On his way out of the condo building, Adrian stopped by the mailboxes **on the first floor** to retrieve his mail. He liked letting the mail build up to at least a week's worth before collecting it. Already standing at the mailboxes was another resident of the high rise who's been trying to get Adrian's attention.

"Hi there," initiated the stranger.

"Hello," Adrian replied.

"I'm Alex. I've seen you working out in the gym **a few** times – you were with another guy." Alex was fishing for any hint of what the relationship status might be between Adrian and Earl.

"Yes. That would be my buddy from college." He purposely withheld Earl's name.

"I see," Alex eyed Adrian from head to toe appreciating the results of his workout regimen. "Maybe we can buddy up sometime."

"Um, sure."

With the precision of a Pez dispenser, Alex retrieved and handed Adrian a business card. Printed on the purple card was [Alex Dancer, coordinator for THE MAIN EVENT PLANNING AGENCY.] "Give me a call, the next time you're going to work out."

"Um, okay."

After retrieving his handful of mail and going to his car, Adrian sat sifting through the envelopes. Standing out from the collection of mail was one oversized red envelope. He knew what was inside the envelope based on the Marion, Indiana return address. It also reminded him of something that he had forgotten.

In the envelope was a greeting card with a child's face on the outside. There were two holes where the child's nose was to be. Printed on the forehead of the child, "*You can't pick your family . . .*" On the inside, the verse continued, "*. . . but you can always pick your nose.*" Enclosed with the card was the usual personal check made out for $25 from his Busia.

Adrian's grandmother was the only person who ritually remembered his birthday. Although, none of his acquaintances, coworkers, or friends knew when his birthday was or bothered to even ask. His sister Katelin did not even have the decency to text him a happy birthday wish. He took a deep breath and failed at holding it in or the tears that welled in his eyes. He let out a whimpering sigh as he smelled the Estee Lauder Youth Dew perfume his Busia always wore.

෧෨෧෨

The waiting room at the OBGYN office was full of women eager to climb in the set of stirrups and spread their legs for the handsome and elusive Dr. Adrian Wiggins, P.A. They prepared for a visit to the gynecologist as if they were going on a date. They were freshly showered – wearing new underwear – their legs shaved or waxed with a spritz of perfume. Cute pedicure as if Adrian were going to notice their toes. That didn't stop them from flirting.

"Hello Miss Johnston," the handsome P.A. greeted the woman who'd been excitedly waiting.

Vagina's **sultry** *voice: "Hello, doooooooctor. Aren't you going to say something about my new hairdo? It's a French bikini wax. I wanted to show you something different than what you're going to see on the rest of those va-jay-jays waiting to get in here. Like it? Oh, and did you notice I'm wearing - lip gloss. Come on, give us a little kiss."*

ॐ◅ॐ◅ॐ

Sitting at his desk, Adrian's cell phone rang with the default whistle ringtone. He looked at the number appearing in the display, recognizing the Indiana 765 area code. Immediately his mind thought the worst. Something must have happened to his grandmother.

"Happy birthday son." By the use of the word son, the **female** caller assumed that it would identify who she was. It was not the voice of the woman who raised him for the past thirty years. It was not the voice of the woman who nurtured and encouraged him. It was not the voice of the woman who had never failed to send him a humorous birthday card with a personal check enclosed. "Hello," stated the caller.

"Yeah, I'm here." Adrian acknowledged.

"I got your number from your sis-sister. I hope **that** was okay."

"Uh, sure . . . no problem." He lied. It was a problem for Adrian. He was in traumatic shock. **He was surprised** that he recognized a voice that he had not heard in his entire adult life. He was upset that he was somewhat excited by the sound of the woman's birthday wish. He was disgusted that he didn't immediately disconnect the call.

"So how've you been?" **She asked.**

Are you f-in kidding me? "Okay."

"That's good to hear. Katlin says you are the doctor for the Real Housewives of Atlanta. That must be exciting. I love watching that show."

Eat shit and die. "Actually, I see lots of patients and I don't pay too much attention to who's who."

"Oh, I see. Your Busia wanted to make sure you got your (awkward pause), birthday card."

SERIOUSLY! You've got some damn nerve lady. "Yes, I did. I opened it this morning. You know, she's given me one every year since I moved to Georgia. Although I never had a birthday party growing up, she made sure I had cake and ice cream on my birthday. Yeah, *SHE* sure did." Finally, Adrian had hoped that his inference spoke his true thoughts.

A soft whimper grew into a sobbing crescendo. It was her, not him, although Adrian was fighting back angry tears. He won the fight.

"Katlin's father left me." *There it is!*

For the next twenty minutes, Adrian's birth mother gave him the Jerry Springer version of the ending of the marriage. She was left struggling financially, having to take a job as an assistant manager at a Wal-Mart Super Center. Trying to get caught up on her bills, she began going to not one, but multiple Pay Day Loan companies. The mother admitted that Katlin told her how generous Adrian had been when she came to him for money. She was now hoping that her son would extend his generosity her way.

"I . . . I . . ." he uttered when a knock was at his office door. "Yes."

"Doctor, your next patient is here," informed the office assistant.

"Thank you." Into the cell phone, "I uh, have to go."

"Sure, sure, I understand. Adrian, I hate to ask, but I was wondering if you could help me out?"

"May I call you back?"

"Sure, . . . **sure**. Anything that you can send would be helpful."

"I'll call you back. I have a patient."

"Right, (*another awkward pause*) Adrian."

"Yeah."

"I love you."

"I have to go."

❧❦❧❦

The office assistant looked at the clipboard on the counter to **remind herself** who was to be seen **next**. "Vera Howard, you can come on back."

Eleven - If Only You Knew.

"Greatness is not determined by what you have but by whom you are and what you do with what you have that helps others." Bishop Dale C.

"The blessed of us are here for the rest of us." Dr. Frederick D. Haynes, III

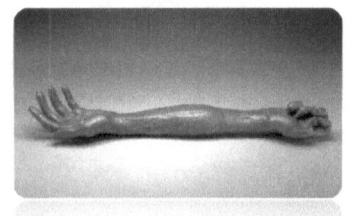

Earl stood at the large dressing table inside his immense walk-in closet. He looked upon the choice of garments to wear on his special date. He had chosen a lavender button-up shirt to wear under a light wool heather gray V-neck sweater paired with fitted brown trousers. He accessorized the attire with a pair of black penny loafers. The loafers were adorned with the current years' penny tucked in the lips. For his distinctive scent for the evening, he chose Hanae Mori HIM over his Tom Ford *Black Orchid* cologne.

The cell phone rang. Earl answered by putting it in speaker mode. "Talk to me."

"Man, you won't believe who had the damn nerve to call me, to wish me a happy birthday." Adrian led in with his conversation.

"Today's your birthday?"

"Yeah, but guess who called me?"

"Happy birthday *bruh*."

"Yeah. Yeah. It was my mother."

Earl was the sole person in Adrian's circle of acquaintances and friends who knew of his family background. He would turn to Earl to vent whenever Katelin would text him asking for money as if he were her ATM. Like any good friend, Earl provided his unabashed words of advice. Adrian could recite them in his head. *"You don't fix money problems with money,"* Earl would offer. *"Helping is what you do when you know good will come out of something. Giving someone anything they want, without working for it is not helping them at all. Instead, it is hurting them and hurting you."*

Adrian gave Earl the Cliff Notes version of his conversation with his mother.

"No, she didn't," Earl uttered in somewhat disbelief.

"Yeah, man. I know what you say about helping, but what should I do?"

"You need to **learn to say 'no' without having to explain**."

"But it's my mother," Adrian admonished with little conviction.

Initially, Earl did not dignify what he just heard with a response.

"Adrian, I'm for helping others in need. But there is something inherently wrong with an absentee parent coming to her abandoned child for money. Something shameful and it's clear that your mother is not embarrassed in the least bit to ask you for it." Earl realized the hypocrisy of his words when he thought of his mother's a whim call to him when she sees the latest and greatest device being advertised by Apple.

"I'm sure it was hard for her." Adrian defended.

"Right, it took her what; thirty-some years to work up the nerve to call you. There comes a time when you have to stop crossing an ocean for people who wouldn't jump over a puddle for you." The silence that followed hinted to Earl that he may have said too much. But he had more advice to give. "Okay, if I were you, I wouldn't send your mother any money. Ask her for the name and addresses of the loan companies and you pay on her accounts directly."

"Is that what you do with your mother?" Adrian **retorted and** thought, "*Touché*."

"As a matter of fact, yes I do. With any bill that I'm paying on behalf of my mother; I have access to it or my name is on the account. With your approach *bruh*, you are hurting your family. This is not about you being a good **son or brother**. This is about them figuring life out for themselves. They are going to keep coming to you with their financial problems, pinching on your money to take care of it. **Family borrows from family because it is the path of least resistance**." Earl offered.

You didn't answer my selfie text, you selfish SOB. "You've got all the answers, don't you? Well not everyone is like Mister Earl Grey. Some of us have feelings and care about others."

"What are you talking about? I care about others."

"You only care about yourself."

"What?!" Earl was surprised by **Adrian's consternation**.

Adrian's emotions and frustration were exposing some deep-seated jealousy he had harbored toward Earl. After knowing him for several years, Adrian knew very little about Earl that was not printed in a magazine or **posted on** his LinkedIn profile. There were also dating rumors posted on *Media Take Out* of Earl with celebrities. **Other than that, he** knew **little** of his personal life, while Earl knew quite a bit about his. Not only that, Adrian suspected that there was indeed someone that Earl confided in – so why not him.

"I'm sorry man. I . . . I'm just a little rattled with my mother calling, that's all. My bad," Adrian apologized.

"It's cool."

"No, really - I'm sorry."

"I understand. It's cool. Hey look, I have to finish getting dressed."

"So what do you have going on this evening?"

"I'm having dinner with a friend."

"With who?"

Adrian was surprised at his asking and so was Earl.

"Fiona," replied Earl.

Hearing her name reignited Adrian's ire. He resented their relationship. Adrian recalled on numerous occasions, Earl had broken workout plans with him because of a pop-in visit by Fiona. Adrian evoked making early morning phone calls to Earl and Fiona would be there. That was a clear indication to him that she had spent the night. Whenever he would ask Earl if there was anything between the two of them, he would emphatically state that they were just friends.

The only comforting and consoling thoughts Adrian had were his assessments of an independent woman like Fiona. There was little chance that she would settle down with just any man - even in his opinion, a renaissance man like Earl Grey. As a backhanded compliment, Adrian felt that she was lyrically the autonomous woman sung about in the song "She Got Her Own" featuring Jamie Foxx and Fabolous.

"Oh," Adrian was feeling more assured.

Unlike women from his mother's era, millennium women like Fiona were becoming **more like** the men they want to marry. Feeling better that his *bromance* with Earl was not threatened; Adrian searched his pockets for his business card Alex Dancer.

❧ ❧ ❧ ❧

Fiona was excitedly fluttering around the bedroom like a **black** butterfly in an open field of tulips. She was getting ready for a dinner date with Earl. They had arranged to meet at the Bahama Breeze Island Grille restaurant near her house. She wasn't sure what excited her more. Was it the anticipated taste of the rice bowl with Mahi & Shrimp with Lemongrass Sauce? The dish reminded her of the Jollof rice dish she ate **growing up** in Africa. Or was it the anticipation of seeing Earl?

Kendra intently watched her friend getting dressed. She sipped a glass of Barefoot Moscato wine, consuming nearly the entire bottle by herself. **The moment** took her back to their **dorm room** days at Spelman. Even though she was from another continent and had trouble putting together conjugal verbs, **back then** Fiona **seemed to have** had a date every weekend. That's because she exuded exotic sensuality. When Fiona spoke the most common phrases with her thick French-**African-laden** accent, she had guys hanging on her every word like puppy dogs on a leash.

Just like it was then, Kendra would **sit** back watching her friend get ready for a night out. Little did Fiona know then that Kendra was not only quite envious but more infatuated with her. The thing that she found attractive about Fiona was that while she was soft, she was so damn aggressive and ambitious.

While the two of them were getting a mani-pedi; an Asian manicurist prophesized to Fiona that her choice of *Squoval*-shaped nails meant that she would be successful in business. Kendra **then** chose the same rounded edges **over** a *squarish* nail style for herself. She felt safe and comfortable when **she was** with Fiona. **Society would**

consider their relationship what would be called a *womance* when speaking about them in public and a lesbian couple when in private.

In college Kendra never had sex with a woman and probably thought she never would. She **had** gently kissed some girls before (and liked it). It wasn't until after she had married that her then-husband persuaded her into engaging in a threesome for his pleasure. While for her husband the sexual liaison satisfied a fantasy, for Kendra it resolved a curiosity. Well, almost. The same-sex encounters triggered desires, images, and memories of Fiona. Now, the memories were no longer needed.

Still damp from her shower, Fiona emerged adorned in an oversized towel which was tightly wrapped around her fit build. Comfortably resting her head against Fiona's king-size headboard Kendra gulped wine. The wine put Kendra in a relaxed and subtle mood. She sized up her friend's physique. Standing, Fiona was five feet four inches tall, curvy back, solid legs, about 160 pounds. Her BMI doesn't match her weight because of the muscle mass that she carries but makes her well-proportioned. She had a head full of thick black naturally wavy hair, with long lashes framing almond-shaped brown eyes and a succulent full bottom lip – her skin a smooth Hershey chocolate-colored delight.

Just when the mildly intoxicated Kendra thought she had compiled a fair assessment, Fiona dropped the towel from around her, revealing a 34-24-36 frame. Kendra gasped. Exposed before her were perky breasts, a slim waistline, and a generously and perfectly round posterior. "Oh yeah; for a taste of that, I would consider becoming a *vaginatarian*," Kendra mentally fancied. She swallowed hard to remove the salivation and cleared her throat to speak.

"You've, *ahem*, you've just come home and now you're going out to dinner," Kendra complained.

"*Oui.*"

"But we haven't had any time to catch up."

"*Je ne comprends pas*. We are talking now."

"You know what I mean."

"I can listen to you and get dressed at the same time. It is called multi-tasking."

"Don't talk to me like I'm stupid," Kendra commanded. "I know what multi-tasking is."

Fiona turned from her closet in Kendra's direction. To be fair, it was the first time Fiona focused on her friend since she arrived home from the airport. She saw Kendra's unkempt hair and her face was without makeup, which was normally well kept. She didn't look like her polished self while wearing Fiona's nightshirt which read; "I run like a girl. Just try to keep up." Fiona joined her friend by sitting on the bed.

"What is up with you *gurl*?" Fiona queried.

"It's just that you always do this. You don't spend any time here. You fly in and go straight to *Euuuuuurrl's* house and you only come here to change clothes and repack. And then you're gone again."

"What are you talking about? You aren't my only friend you know," Fiona offered in an attempt to console, "but you are my best friend." She added with a genuine smile acutely empathetic of Kendra's distress. She placed her hand gently atop Kendra's.

It worked. Kendra's visage softened. Her eyes dilated, her heart lightened and her pulse quickened. Fiona was glad that she was able to make her friend feel better. Peering back at Fiona, she looked her deeply in the eyes. Suddenly Fiona felt naked.

"Okay, now I got to go or I'll be late." Fiona bounced off the bed and resumed getting dressed.

Earl was already seated at the restaurant, sipping on a margarita when Fiona arrived at Bahama Breeze. Escorted to the table by the hostess, Fiona carried a large tin canister of Garrett's popcorn, The Chicago Mix. She presented the canister to Earl before giving him a full-body hug.

"Sorry, I'm late. I almost got a speeding ticket getting 'ere." Fiona explained.

"How do you almost get a ticket?"

"The policeman said 'e would let me go this time if I gave 'im my number so that 'e could call me. 'ow do you say, 'Quid pro quo?'"

"Yes, something like that. So what's this?" Earl asked while holding the obviously marked popcorn tin.

"It's for you, for being my friend."

"Well, thank you."

The couple chit-chatted over appetizers and entrees about what had transpired in their lives, both personally and professionally since the last time they spoke. Best friends. Good friends. Old friends. For dessert, they shared a Banana Nut Bread Supreme and stories that caught them up on their day's event.

"Hey, let me tell you what happened right before I left home," Earl stated.

"Sure."

Earl tells her about the phone conversation with Adrian. He didn't disclose the details of Adrian's relationship with his mother. He did repeat the advice that he offered Adrian when it came to him helping his family financially. "Borrowing and lending can spoil relationships." Earl provided. He looked upon his relationship with Fiona as the exception with her having paid back all of the money she ever borrowed.

Fiona was in agreement that his advice was sound. She even saw how she could use it in dealing with those who called on her for money. "The Swahili say; 'borrowing is like a wedding; repaying is like mourning,'" she conveyed.

"Okay, well I thought I was trying to be helpful. Although he later apologized, my boy did sound seriously agitated."

"I'm sure it was just; what do you say, *querelle d'amoureux*."

"Come again?"

". . . just *eh*, a lover's spat."

"A what?"

"Oh, you 'ave to know that 'e likes you."

"What are you talking about?"

"You men are so blind at times. The first time I saw you two, I thought you were a couple. Remember when we met at Whole Foods?"

Earl recalled the first time he laid eyes on Fiona at the supermarket chain that specializes in selling organic products. He and Adrian had stopped in the store to get a Power Shot from their juice bar of wheatgrass, fresh ginger, and lemon juice, sprinkled with cayenne pepper. Earl decided to purchase a box of his namesake Earl Grey tea when he beheld a profile view of Fiona wearing a pair of jeggings in heels and a t-shirt. The two struck up a conversation when she mentioned that she favored the Lady Grey variation of the tea.

He was awestruck. She put him in mind of the actress Tika Sumpter, with her bronze skin tone beauty. From his view of her physique, he saw lovely opulent curves. His eyes were drawn particularly to her visible panty line creasing into her soft flesh. Adrian, on the other hand, saw her visibly as dangerous curves ahead.

"You thought we were a couple?" Earl asked astounded.

"Well . . . I mean a nice-looking couple." She followed with a smile.

"Really," shaking his head. "That's just like me saying that you and Kendra are a couple."

"Yeah right," she scoffed, and they both laughed. Fiona flashed back to the last conversation with Kendra and the look in her eyes. She then gave thought to her other girlfriends.

"Kendra is like most of my other girlfriends, although most of them are older than 'er or I. They all complain that I don't spend more time with them. They play tug-of-war with me. This is why I like 'anging out at your 'ouse as a *pied-à-terre*. They can't find me and I can avoid answering my phone."

"Oh, so you're using my house to hide out."

"You know I like spending time with you." She reached over and covered his hand with hers. "With them, it's kind of crazy. Like now, we're supposed to be going to the Beyoncé and Jay-Z concert. But one friend won't go if another one does. They call each other names like *bitches* and *ratchet*."

Fiona went on to provide examples of the playful but sometimes intense infighting between her girlfriends. As she spoke, Earl ruminated about what he learned of Fiona's character and lifestyle. He peered into the face of the attractive young woman sitting across the table. For the first time, he noticed an old scar above her upper lip – making a mental note to ask her how she got it. He guessed that it came from her falling out of a tree that she climbed as a tomboy child.

This was the woman that he knew to be smart, sociable, and spiritual by nature. Over the years of the friendship, Earl grew to love Fiona. He trusted her and her faithfulness to their friendship to give her possession of a key to his house. Unbeknownst to her, she possessed the key to his heart as well; though it was obvious to him that she did not need him as her mate. Fiona had become the mate he wanted and needed. Instead of acknowledging it, he numbed his heart toward her to guard his feelings against being hurt.

"Enough about them . . . Babe, I want to show you Punta Cana." She stated with a disarming and inviting smile.

Earl searched his little gray cells for any foreign or slang reference to what he mistook for a coy euphemism. "Ooookay, I never heard it called that before. Soooo, your place or mine?"

"You're so silly." She followed with a chuckle. "Punta Cana is at the eastmost tip of the Dominican Republic. So I want to take you there. *Mon traitement.* My treat."

"What?" Earl was conditionally and traditionally old school. Accepting a tin of popcorn was one thing. In the past he had accepted small endearing gifts from Fiona; handmade bath scrub scented with patchouli oil, hibiscus tea with rose petals. Allowing a woman to pay for a Caribbean cruise trip was another. It gave him a flashback to when he was courting Greedy. Although Earl was assured when it came to him that Fiona was not looking for a Captain Save 'Em.

"*Oui.* You and me on the beach with the wide-open sea."

"And why this, Punny . . ."

"Punta Cana." Fiona corrected. "I met this guy named Abayomi on the flight 'ome and 'e was telling me about it. 'e'd just come from there and asked me if I would like to go back with 'im. 'e gave me this." She reached in her purse and pulled out a half-eaten Kah Kow chocolate candy bar.

"I don't know what to say." His mind was crossed between wariness and wantonness.

"You say 'yes,' no."

"I don't know that I can say yes. It's not that easy."

"Why for?"

"For one thing; you know I usually vacation with my mother every year."

"Bring 'er."

Earl was not expecting that response from her. "Uh, let me get back to you on that."

❧❧❧❧❧

"Alex, it's Adrian. We spoke earlier in the lobby. I was wondering if you would like to meet up for coffee at the Octane Coffee bar in Midtown."

Twelve - Why I Did Get Married.

"Sometimes doing what's right is painful and doing what's wrong feels good."

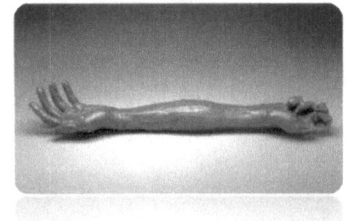

Early Saturday morning came with pouring liquid sunshine. The heavy rainfall began around two a.m. Deshaun was just getting to bed. He couldn't explain it, but the sound of the raindrops on the roof put him in a **lovemaking** mood. He lay beside Vera who was sound asleep. Spooning behind her, he reached around **and** cupped the D-cup breasts beneath the thinly cotton material of her nightgown. He groped and kneaded until he stirred up an affectionate response from his wife.

Blood rushed through Vera's body stimulated by Deshaun's open mouth kisses passionately placed on the back of her neck **and behind her earlobe.** She heard the sound of the rain and found it **arousing** and **seducing.** Whether it was the rain or the warmth of Deshaun's breath, Vera was a favorably respondent **offering a simple request,** "*Suavemente besame, Carino.*" It meant "Gently, kiss me, love." The act of intercourse soon followed.

Ya visto. Deshaun stood at his bedroom window, peering out at his suburban neighborhood. Three and four-bedroom homes with manicured lawns were being washed and watered by the steady falling rain. With the rain, there was a welling of satisfaction of gaining a successful social status. He felt that he **had** made it out of the barrel of his past **poverty** life. His mother **Cusseta** Howard would have been proud of him.

He turned **to look** at his wife asleep, as she was lying across the bed snoring. Just like days before, Deshaun stared at a woman he had just bedded and felt a sense of shame that he did not know the woman very well. What he knew about Vera was based on the time together during their senior year in college, and what she shared of a vague and sketchy past. He did not remember her school major, her career goal, or dreams if she had any.

After a quick shower, Deshaun went downstairs to join the other tenants of his **boarding** household. Sitting at the breakfast table was Eddie, rolling coins and stuffing them in money wrappers. Misunderstanding the concept behind putting coins in wrappers, he stuffed as many as he could in a sleeve before taping the ends closed. He thought the more he could get in the **coin** sleeve, the heavier it would make them and that the **exchange** value would **be greater** based on their weight. He did not ask and no one told him otherwise. His purpose for wrapping the coins instead of taking them to the cash converting CoinStar Kiosks was to be able to keep as much of the money as he could **acquire**.

"G'morning." Deshaun announced himself to the people in the room.

"Hey, Deshaun, what it do?" Eddie greeted his brother-in-law.

"Morning."

"Can I borrow your car to run to the bank to cash these in?"

"Have you paid your fine to get your license renewed?"

"*Whatchu* think I'm trying to do?"

"Then the answer is no."

"You trippin' De'. That's why *hermano* can't come up. Nobody wanna help."

Deshaun dismissed the comment and turned his attention to his son who was sitting across the table from Eddie. "Morning Bradley," he extended. The youth didn't raise his eyes from his cellphone but offered an uptick of his head.

"If you're taking Eddie to the bank, can you take me by the phone store so that I can exchange my phone?" Bradley asked, still without looking at his father.

"Who said that I was taking him to the bank?"

"I'm just asking."

"And didn't your mother just upgrade your phone?"

"Yeah, but the screen got cracked."

"You dropped it **again**?"

"It fell."

"You dropped it."

"Whatever."

Mama Maria was unloading the dishwasher while preparing breakfast. Though it was never spoken aloud, she had become the **live-in** housekeeper of the Howard house. She cooked, cleaned, and picked up behind grandson Bradley, while she fussed at her son Eddie for not picking up behind himself.

"Is Vera comin' down for breakfast?" **Mama** Maria asked.

"I don't know. She was asleep when I left her." Deshaun answered.

"Bradley, go see if your mother wants some eggs and Chorizo sausage?" **Mama** Maria requested.

"He said she was sleeping." Bradley snapped back.

"GO!" She commanded.

The youth snatched his body out of the chair and headed for the stairs. Making it halfway up the flight of stairs, "MA, YOU WANT BREAKFAST," the annoyed boy shouted.

&⁊⛯⛯⚬⛯৯

Life is stranger than fiction.

Everyone in the Howard-Diaz household had gathered in the family room after repeated attempts by Eddie and Bradley to be chauffeured about had failed. The two young men sat feeling dejected as one stared aimlessly at the television, while the other was with his head down focused on his phone. Vera with a glass of homemade Sangria and Deshaun with his brandy sat on opposite ends of the sectional couch. **Mama** Maria was in a chair content while watching her DVR-recorded episodes of Tyler Perry's primetime soap opera "*The Haves and Haves Nots* (HAHNs)."

While the television **HAHNs** cast ran their lines; the family room group quietly reflected on the parts of their life drama. For Maria Diaz, it seemed all too real. From the moment the HAHN's maid Celine's character appeared on the show, Maria had been thinking of how to sue the real-life Wellingtons and Tyler Perry. She had signed a nondisclosure agreement with the Wellingtons, not to discuss the terms of her reemployment as their housekeeper and their condition to pay for Vera's and Eddie's homeschooling and full college tuition. Maria held up her end of the agreement. Not even her children knew what fully transpired between Maria, the Wellingtons, and their legal counsel.

What Vera did know was that the early days of her youth were traumatic. Being separated from her mother, living homeless, and being put into foster care at an early age still haunted her. In a **short amount of time,** she had to grow up way too fast and be the **fill-in** mother to her baby brother. Being reunited with her family and then living a seemingly lavished life in the Wellingtons guest house did help with the emotional healing.

Going from one extreme to the other manifested the "Keeping up with the Joneses" personality in her current lifestyle. It was also why Bradley has had the best Deshaun's money can buy. **Vera** vowed that he would never know what it means to *have not* or **to have** to settle for less.

Deshaun took a glance over at his son. Bradley was consumed in his world of wants and desires. He was a classic example of the millennium entitlement generation. When criticized for his "me" attitude, his typical response was "I didn't ask to be born." He **revered** his parents as his personal "Make a Wish Foundation." But, he was not totally to blame for his insolence. His parents had made every effort to make sure that their son had not needed for anything. Their misguided love was to make sure that he had a better life than they did as a child.

Instead of rearing their son to be a contribution to society, he will likely be a burden to some woman whom he will view as someone who is supposed to take care of him. **In his opinion, the** job that he may get will never pay him enough and to him, they will expect too much for the pay he would receive. And life, in general, will not be fair if he isn't getting **things** his way.

Living in the lap of luxury did **not** sit well with **Eduardo.** It was as if he rebelled from the day **they** moved **into** the Wellingtons' guest house and was **exposed** to whatever they had to offer. Although he took whatever was given to him, he also took as much as he could get away with stealing. There was no explanation for it. Someone called him a "bad seed" just before he was taken away by the police. **Once** again he was placed in foster care by the Division of Family and Children Services.

Eddie remained in foster care until he aged out at the age of eighteen. From then, Eddie hustled his way through life. He met young and old women who had low self-esteem issues who fell prey to him and who were vulnerable to being easily seduced by a young good looking, smooth-talking Latino Casanova.

Deshaun not being a fan of the primetime soap opera HAHNs, he did not know the characters or the show's plot. The same applied to the other males living under the Howard roof. Looking around the family room at the faces, he felt like a stranger in his own home. He got up and refreshed his drink. No one appeared to have noticed his movements as he exited the room.

The stranger in the house went and sat in his car in the attached garage to call his friend.

"What'sup EG?"

"Working. I guess no golf for you today with all this rain?"

"Yeah, it looks like it's going to be a washout for today. *Whatchu* working on?"

"I have a webinar next week. I'm on a panel of speakers being interviewed."

"Okay, that's what's up. I'll let you go then."

"No, it's cool. Talk to me. So what are you and the family up to?"

Deshaun tried his best to express his feeling of isolation in his crowded house. At the same time, he attempted to keep a sense of manhood and not be embarrassed about the situation. His biggest concern was not having control.

"I'm not saying I'm trying to be king of the castle, *knowwhatI'msayin'*. It's just when I come home, I feel like I **got** to tiptoe around these people. It's like I'm living with them, instead of the other way around."

"You shouldn't be made to feel that way in your own home De'. Who's paying the **mortgage?** How much are they contributing to the expenses?"

"Well, nobody **is** really. Her people have their own money so they not cost me much."

"So you're not getting any help on the utilities from your in-laws?"

"No."

"De', as long as they're turning on a light **switch** and flushing a toilet, they're costing you something."

"You funny EG," Deshaun **followed with a** chuckled out loud.

"I'm serious De'."

"*Mane*, you know my situation. Her mom moved in with us to help out with Bradley **when we needed it.**"

"He's now what, fifteen?"

"I know. I know, *mane*."

"How does Vera feel about it?"

"We don't **really** talk about it. She **gets** angry when I bring it up. She say's 'It's my *madre*. You don't know what we've been through.'"

"Been through, like what?" Earl asked.

"I don't know. I just leave it alone, *cuz* she starts crying and shit. I know we should honor our parents and they did a lot for us when we were young."

"There is a very simple way to deal with this. The next time you two **pay** your bills..."

"Vera handles the bills."

"Okay, first of all, you should be **paying the household expenses** together; to track where *your* money goes. I use this website **and app Mint.com**. Online I can see where my money is being spent from every **bank** account, personal or business. It tracks my spending by category, so I can see the trend of spending **on** eating out, groceries, and utilities. These are areas I'm sure your in-laws are contributing. You can also identify unnecessary expenses, and discuss which ones to cut.

"By you doing this together shows that you're trying to look out for your family's financial stability and future, and especially for Bradley; the person you were supposedly serving by having your mother-in-law move in. How much are you putting away for his college?"

"We got some savings. I don't know how much though."

"You should know that or at least be able to find out at the click of a few buttons. We're talking about my godson."

"I hear you *mane.*"

"As for your brother-in-law . . ."

"Don't even get me started." Deshaun was exasperated.

After Deshaun lamented on some of the antics of his freeloading brother-in-law, Earl explained more about the **internet** online financial tracking **website**/application. He informed me, once signed up by adding all of their financial institutes and accounts from banking, credit cards, and investments; that the program would instantly retrieve historical activity.

"Every debit card swipe and **every** check **that was** written would be shown."

"That's **what's up.**" Deshaun acknowledged and appreciated the enlightenment from his friend.

Thirteen - A Better You, Makes a Better We.

"Live up to your potential, not down to others' expectations." *Michael Faulkner*

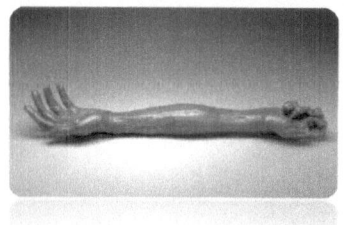

In the break room of St. Have Mercy Hospital, **LPN** Earlene Grey had as many of her coworkers as she possibly could, to gather around a center table. All week she had been **announcing** that her son was going to be on the "internet **channel." She** had the brand-new Sony Xperia Tablet **device propped up in its stand** setup for viewing. In honor of the event, she bought two Crowd Pleaser Party meat and cheese trays **from The Anderson store.** Many of the hospital staff had congregated, some who did not know Earlene by name. Free food gets an audience every time.

Host: "This week on BigMarker.com, we are streaming live, interviews with a few leading professionals in the field of brand management. Today, they are here to speak on the topic of Professional Development and Networking. Our panelists include Keshia Nichole Walker, owner of Insights Marketing & Promotions Company, Reggie **Hayman**, Business/Career Consultant, and Earl Grey, Brand Strategist and Principal of It's Me, Inc."

"There's my baby." Earlene **broadcasted** to **her** over-the-shoulder onlookers.

The **online** host opened with "Ladies first; **so Miss Walker** let's start with you."

"Don't nobody want to hear her." Earlene spewed. A few chuckles came from around the room.

Host: "Keshia, what are **your** five keys to **making** it in this industry and breaking through the glass ceiling?"

Walker: "I like to call **them** the five Ps. They are **prayer**, first and foremost, **then persistence, patience, preparation,** and being in the right **place** at the right time."

After Walker expounded on seeing women branch out and start their businesses and keeping great connections, Reggie **Hayman** was next to be interviewed. Earlene let a few expletives loose. More chuckles filled the break room. By the time it was Earl's opportunity to speak, many of the **gatherers** had eaten and gone.

Host: "Earl Grey, bestselling author, and personal/professional brand champion. How are you?"

Grey: "I'm well, thank you."

Host: "I'd say, before we get to the interview; social media rumors have you dating R&B singer Chrisette Michele and **a** former Atlanta Falcon cheerleader."

Grey: "No comment."

Host: "Okay. Okay. That wasn't fair. This isn't TMZ **after all**. Let's go back to the beginning of your career successes. You started an ad guy."

Grey: "Yes. I worked for L.C. Arts and Advertising. I started there as a Graphic Design intern and later I was hired. It was my high school art teacher, Miss Shelby at Jesup W. Stuart who got me interested in graphic design. She had me enter a contest to draw an ad to go on the city's OARTA buses. I won."

Host: "When I said let's go back, you went all the way back."

Grey: "Teachers deserve a lot of credit."

Host: "As an ad guy you were on the fast track. At the American Advertising Federation Convention someone introduced you as the 'golden boy with the Midas touch.'"

Grey: "Let's just say I helped clients to put a gold shine on their products."

Host: "Can you tell us how?" (A slight pause.)

Grey: "Well, it came from my childhood..."

Earlene "*shh*" the people in the room - anticipating hearing from her son "I owe it all to my mother."

Grey: "I was raised by a single mother. We didn't have much money when I was growing up. When we went shopping at the A&P grocery store, we could only afford the generic brand of the can and dry goods. They were unmistakably wrapped with a black and white label or box." He chuckled and shook his head. "Not only was I embarrassed when my friends would see what was in our shopping cart, but the contents of those products were also pretty bad. Like, in a can of green beans - they would have stem pieces inside and who knows what else."

Host: "That's scary."

Grey: "Well, when I got in the position to make a difference, I approached national chain stores and told them my generic brand experience. I was able to show them how to create their store brands to be competitive with nationally known brands. I was able to convince them that there will always be people to buy the off brands if you will."

Host: "So you made lemonade out of lemons."

Grey: "Figuratively, I suppose so."

Earlene Grey's mouth fell open and if it were possible, she would have liked to have disappeared in a puff of smoke from embarrassment.

Host: "In your book, A Better You; you put a different spin on 'paying it forward.' You say one should 'pay it backward.' Would you explain what you mean by that?"

Grey: "Sure, let me explain my thinking when I wrote that of the book. I don't necessarily subscribe to the traditional concept of paying it forward, because of what it does to the person receiving a random act of kindness. That person is sort of obligated by the giver to bestow a kind act on to someone else. Pay-it-forward. So, so two things; one, I shouldn't obligate someone else to be kindhearted. Either you're going to do it or you're not; based on your personal and moral convictions. And two, I say pay it backward as in reach back to the person coming behind you trying to get where you are or that generation of people who are going to contribute to the future."

Host: "Okay, I can agree with that. What is your definition of a personal brand?"

Grey: "That's an easy one. And I can't take full credit for this definition. I borrowed it from Gandhi, who said that 'happiness is when what you think, what you say, and what you do are in harmony.' Your personal brand consists of three things, what you think, say, and do. That is who you are, and your brand pure and simple. The magic is to project the best of you and your brand."

Host: "As you said, simple. One last question; what inspires you to show up to work each day?"

Grey: "A long time ago someone once quoted to me that, 'if you're the smartest person in the room then it's time to leave the room.' I'd like to think that if I find myself the smartest person in the room, then it's upon me to teach those in the room with me."

Host: "With that Mister Grey, you get the last word. That concludes our webcast and I'd like to thank each of today's guests. Look for more webinars on Personal Development and Networking on BigMarker.com"

ॐ◦ॐ◦ॐ◦ॐ

"How could you embarrass ME like that; telling the whole world that we were poor?" Earlene protested to her son.

"Mom, I did not say we were poor. I said we struggled financially, which was true."

"Do you have any idea how you made ME look in front of all my coworkers and friends?"

"Will you please stop shouting? What I said was ger*mane* to the story about my background."

"Who is Jermaine? Is he the guy that was asking the questions?"

"No, that was . . . never mind."

"And, you didn't even thank your mother like that basketball player did on T.V., who made everybody cry."

"Mom, I thank you all the time."

"But not in front of people. You owe me for bringing you up the right way and keeping **your ass** out of trouble."

"You're my mother; that's what you were supposed to do."

"Un-*unh*, I could have let you run around with that Deshaun boy and who knows where you would have ended up."

"Deshaun is **now** married with a kid, working and doing fine."

"You remember that his mother got kilt 'cause she was still living in those projects. That's before the city finally tore them down."

"Yes, ma'am. I was at the funeral."

"My goodness, who knows what people are saying about me at the hospital."

"What do you care what people say about you?"

"I need to go on vacation. Where are we going this year? I hope it's somewhere really nice. That way I can take some nice pictures and show people when I get back."

"Yeah, well about that."

Earl told his mother that he was possibly vacationing with a friend and that she would not be joining them. Name-calling immediately commenced by his mother; "you good-for-nothing," "selfish," "ungrateful," along with a few obscene words were exchanged. Earlene got off the phone in an ugly mood. Earl, on the other hand, was relieved to his core being. He finally pushed back to his mother. The cost; mother and son would not speak with one another for quite some time.

"Look mom; I've got places to go, people to see, and things to do and not necessarily in that order." Earl ended the call.

Needless to say, there was no vacation or port of call cruise to Punta Cuna for Earl, Fiona or Earlene. Earlene took off a week from work, spending it in Detroit while telling her friends and coworkers that she was going on an exotic vacation. As for Fiona, she accepted the offer of the airplane passenger who bestowed her with the chocolate candy bar.

"EG, IT'S DESHAUN; DO YOU KNOW WHAT THAT CRAZY-ASS WOMAN DID? SHE GAVE THAT CHURCH ALL OUR SAVINGS. YOU BETTER GET OVER HERE QUICK BECAUSE SOMEBODY IS GOING TO JAIL OR TO GRADY HOSPITAL."

Fourteen – As Time Goes By

"What's done in the dark will come to light."

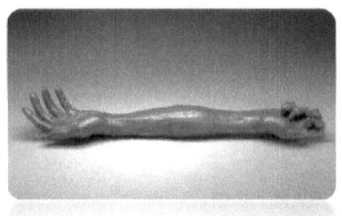

"Thanks for letting me stay **at your crib**." Deshaun expressed gratitude to Earl.

"No problem *bruh*."

"*Mane*, I just lost it. That crazy bitch . . ."

"Hey! Hey! Come on De'. There's no cause for that."

"NO CAUSE! She gave away five G's of my money to that pimp in the pulpit. I'm not *rolling* like you. They still taking money out of my paycheck **from** when I took that loan out **of** my four-oh-one-K, to pay for my mother's funeral."

"Still, be cool with the name-calling." Earl had a sudden aversion to cursing after the recent bout with his mother. "You're not going to like hearing this, but you're partly to blame, *bruh*."

"WHAT? How you figure?"

"You should have been more involved with what was going on with you all's finances."

"You mean MY money."

"No, *y'alls* money. You may bring in the bulk of the income, but she does have some money coming in. And because you're married, do I need to remind you that you're considered as one."

"That SSD check she gets don't pay for shit."

"That's a different issue. Especially with you being the man of the house, you should know what's going on. I'm not saying that you should be controlling but be aware and y'all should be in agreement." Earl put on the brakes by laying the blame on Deshaun as he remembered that his friend never had a good example of what it meant to be *a man of the house*. "You see what using Mint.com showed you, right?"

"Yeah, you right about that shit. I really didn't know how much money she been spending at the mall on her and Bradley."

There was a silence that lasted for seemingly much longer than the actual moment. The only sound came from Deshaun's squirming against Earl's Corinthian leather couch. With his head hung deep into his chest, he cleared his throat to speak.

"Hey EG."

"Yeah."

"*Mane*, I messed up."

"You'll be able to work it out."

"*Nah, nah*; I'm not talking about the money, shit."

"Then what?"

"I think I got something."

"What do you mean, got something?"

"My shit burns when I piss. I think I caught somethin'."

"What!?! You better get your butt off my couch!"

❧✦❧✦❧

"*A recent government report reveals some shocking statistics about sexual health in America alleging that hundreds of thousands of Americans are walking around with a sexually transmitted disease and don't even know it!*" - From 2007 to 2012 National Health and Nutrition Examination Survey

Adrian Wiggins, PA continued to read that *the Study claims over 400,000 cases of undiagnosed chlamydia in America. Although millions of dollars are spent each year to promote safe sex, the rate of sexually transmitted diseases continues to rise across the country. According to the CDC, individuals between the ages of 15 and 24 represent half of the new STD cases. Women under 25 are recommended to be tested for chlamydia every year. The most common STDs include chlamydia, gonorrhea, and syphilis. Consistent condom use and practicing monogamy can decrease the likelihood of catching an STD. The state of Georgia ranked third amongst 10 states where it's easiest to catch an STD; 534 per 100,000 have chlamydia. It ranks 5th in gonorrhea and 1st in syphilis transmissions.*

"Doctor, your next patient is in exam room one, and here's her file."

"Thanks, **Sasha**." Adrian acknowledged the medical assistant.

❧✦❧✦❧

"Misses Howard, I have your test results. And it appears that you've contracted an STD; specifically, chlamydia," Adrian informed his patient. "The good news is I'm going to prescribe an oral antibiotic. A single dose of azithromycin twice daily for seven to fourteen days should clear it right up."

No response came from wife and mother Vera Howard.

"Now, we do suggest that you inform anyone that you may have had sexual relationships and ask them to see their physician to be checked as well. Do you have any questions?"

Vera's vagina voice: *"What!? You've never* **seen** *an angry one before. You damn skippy I'm angry. Look at me; I'm drooling, and my breath stank. Oh, I'm not mad at 'chu. I know exactly who I'm going to TELL to get his ass checked out. Gave me this crap . . . Acho men. Hijo de la gran puta.!"*

ॐॐॐ

"Merde!" swore **Fiona**, as she continued to lament to Earl about Kendra moving out of the house unannounced and taking some of **Fiona's belongings** – designer purses and shoes. *"Sacre Bleu!* 'ow could she do this to me? I was 'er friend **who** took 'er in when she 'ad no place to go."

Kendra was not answering her cell phone. She could not answer the phone number Fiona had for her because that number was no longer in service, which was not a surprise. Every six months or so, Kendra would have a new cell phone number with a different carrier. **This was a tactic** to avoid paying a **past due** bill and to evade debt collectors. Earl sensed that Fiona was more hurt by the betrayal and broken trust than the loss of her **possessions. So he** didn't interrupt her vent with his opinion.

Now wasn't the time for him to be the voice of reason and to **cite** the limitations of the law. Both voices would not **have been** saying anything in Fiona's favor on regaining her property and getting justice by taking Kendra to small claims court. Fiona would not likely want to hear from Earl; "here's my credit card, go shopping at Lennox Mall or Phipps Plaza." Instead, he simply listened.

During Fiona's exorcise, she disclosed that her other girlfriends seemed to be of the opinion that Kendra was not a friend at all, but a user. They were also all in favor of enacting their brand of justice.

"She's ratchet, is all."

"Some people think of themselves as chilled champagne in a tall glass when in reality they're lukewarm piss in a plastic cup."

"I think her ass was jealous of you."

"Nah, something else was going on with that chick. I know someone who works for APD and he can track her down."

"My auntie Snap has some two-dollar people who will find her and will *beat* her natural ass."

The last comment brought a chuckle out loud from Earl. He made a serious mental note about the two-dollar people just in case he may one day need the use of their services. "You never know," he thought to himself.

Being reared to be a provider and now in a profession as a solution giver, maybe was the time for Earl to mention something that he had heard on one of his choice television ministries; "God doesn't remove problems from your life, He removes the people who cause the problems. And it is our discernment to not chase after what He has chased away."

"Listen to Fiona; cutting people out of your life doesn't mean that you have to hate them. It simply means that you respect yourself by doing so." Earl continued.

Fiona seemed to take the words to heart and soul.

Fifteen – Private Conversations amongst Friends

"Share the burden. Don't take on the load."

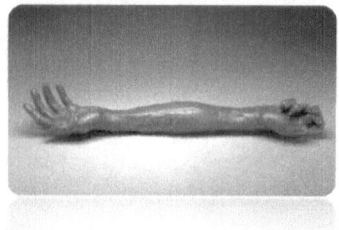

Early fall temperatures crept into the summer of North Georgia. The mornings began cool, the days grew comfortable and the nights settled gorgeously. It was a Saturday evening, 82 degrees, with clear skies with light winds. It turned out to be a perfect night for a dinner party.

It was a surprise premiere launch party being held in Earl's house. The mailed invitations were sent by AT, his business manager to his close circle of friends and business partners. A private cook was hired along with a wait staff to serve asparagus, baby beets, spring greens, new potatoes, mixed vegetables, teriyaki glazed salmon, and lean meats. For dessert Maple-Rum strawberries with vanilla frozen yogurt and oven-baked banana pudding with a meringue topping. The table wine was an Argentinian Malbec.

Earl asked Cynthia Anita-Simone Henderson, his financial and spiritual advisor to say grace to those gathered around the two marble-topped islands in the kitchen. *"Before this table of prepared nourishment; Father, we recognize you as our LORD and Savior. You are the owner of everything. We recommit ourselves to your Lordship. We thank you for our host this evening.*

"We ask that by your Spirit; restrain us from the fleshly impulses of our eyes, flesh, and pride of life that so easily lure us into debt. Teach us how to be content with who we are and what we have and not become influenced by the propaganda of this culture.

"Help us to be a faithful steward in our sowing, spending, and saving of the monies you have entrusted to us. Free us from all guilt and shame of past mistakes and enable us to see the bright future. I thank you now for the Victory! In Jesus Christ's name, I pray. Amen!"

The other guests except for Deshaun joined with an "Amen." The Howards felt some *kind* of *way* that the prayer asks were targeted toward them. Both Deshaun and Vera shot darted gazes toward Earl as they raised their heads. He was innocent of their suspicion that he had told Cynthia of their financial misfortunes though her being invited to the dinner was intentional. Adrian and Fiona also sensed the blessing was oddly conspicuous, taking in mind their financial misgivings.

After dinner, Earl made his way around his home greeting guests.

"Mister Earl, *whassup*" his godson Bradley greeted him with a modicum of respect.

"I'm well. Are you enjoying yourself?" Earl replied.

"It's *aight*."

"Don't you mean it's alright?"

"Yeah. It's alright. Hey, I *betcha* have side-chicks checkin' in and out of here like a Holiday Inn, huh?"

"Uh, no. I think you know me better than that."

"Yeah, but man, you could."

"It's not about the **number** of women; it's about the quality of the woman."

"Oh, I already know. **The** woman I'm *goin'ta* get with; I've seen her."

"Really. Do tell."

"We went to the bank so my uncle Eddie could cash in some change. So we were early **right** before the bank had opened. That's when I saw her. She was dressed all professional-like and she pulled out the keys to the front door. The woman I'm going to marry is going to be like her and have the keys to the bank."

Earl chuckled a bit.

"What?" the youth asked.

"Nothing **really**; you just amaze me **sometimes**. By the way, do you know who else **might have** a key to the bank?"

"Who?"

"**Maybe a** woman who **owns and operates the** cleaning crew."

"Yeah right. Ha, ha, that's a good one Mister Earl."

࿐⚜⚜࿐

Earl made his way **through** the dining room to the outside deck to find his best friend Deshaun, his wife, and mother-in-law. He **fist-bumped** with Deshaun and hugged and kissed Vera and **Mama** Diaz.

"How's my favorite family?" asked Earl. He didn't **expect** to **hear** the details of their family and marriage counseling sessions, which took a great deal of convincing on his part to get **the Howards** to attend.

"We're good." "It's alright." "Fine," were their **respective** responses?

"I'm mad *atchu* señor Earl," Maria Diaz proclaimed.

"Why, what did I do?"

"It's what *chu* didn't do. Why didn't *chu* hire me to do *hor* party?"

"Mama Maria, I'm going to tell you the same thing I told my housekeeper Consuela over there; 'how are you going to be my guest if you're working for me.'"

"You still should have hired me. And as for Consuela, I will show her *de* door and *den* I will come in." Mama Maria quipped.

"That won't be necessary, I'm quite happy with her."

"Well okay, but *chu* let me know if she does not make *chu* happy." she winked at Earl.

"Mama Maria, could you excuse us for a minute. I want to talk with these two in private."

Deshaun and Vera followed Earl to his office, where once they all entered, he closed the door behind them.

"Vera, your mother is something else," Earl stated. "Please, have a seat."

"Tell me about it."

"EG, why you call us in here like we're being called into old dude Broadnax's office?"

The trio chuckled out loud with flashbacks to their days together at the Atlanta University Center.

"It's nothing like that De', man. I just wanted to know if the parents of my godson are okay."

"Yeah, I think we good, *mane*. But I can only speak for myself. I admitted that I was wrong in what I did and I owned up to that."

Deshaun sheepishly confessed out loud and before God. Vera nodded in agreement and acceptance. "The counselor said that what we both did was acting out about some other stuff that was bothering us. We weren't dealing with the real issues. For me, I wasn't happy with things at home." He ended his confessional with a sideways look at Vera as if that was her cue.

"What? Why are we tellin' him our business?" Vera protested.

"Hey, hey, you don't have to tell me anything." Earl specified.

"Why not?" Deshaun defended. "I owned up to what I did. You just mad because the counselor called you out on what you were doing. She said a lot of the couples she talks to have – what did she call it, uh, money cheating."

"Financial infidelity," Vera corrected her husband.

"Yeah, that's it. That's where someone starts hiding money from the other person or when they buy stuff and they don't let the other person know about it."

"Basically," Vera interjected, "what she was trying to tell me was that money only buys so much and that it can't buy happiness. And that we need to openly communicate about everything, especially when it comes to money."

Earl's recalled his money manager mentioning similar points about married or unmarried people who combined their finances. More money does not mean happily ever after. An overwhelming majority of couples who have been deceptive about their finances and spending say their actions affected their relationships.

"Right," Deshaun punctuated.

"AND, which spouse brought in more money didn't matter. Respect for one another is what matters. She gave me this book to read called *Happy Wives Club*. It's a good book." Vera openly admitted.

"Yeah, she said people need to stop letting that 'Real Housewife' bullshit from filling their heads about what's happenin' in reality TV life and not *real* life," Deshaun exclaimed in a falsetto pitch. The trio passed quizzical looks between them.

Earl opened the center drawer of his executive desk and retrieved an envelope. He tapped it several times on the desk as if to settle the contents. Handing it to Deshaun, his eyes were on Vera. In the No. 10 size business envelope was a check for five thousand dollars made out to Mr. and Mrs. Deshaun Howard.

"What's this *mane*? We can't take this." Deshaun mildly objected.

"Whatchu mean we can't?!" Vera vehemently rebutted after looking at the personal check.

"I saw on the news what's happening at New Breath Baptist Church with the whole Ponzi scheme scandal. I hope you guys are a part of the civil suit. If you recoup your money, consider this a loan and if not, it's a gift." Earl declared.

Also enclosed in the envelope was a promissory note for them to sign, stipulating those very terms if they chose to accept them. He learned **not to lend money to family and friends out of emotion, but rather with financial wisdom**.

The couple smiled and held each other's hands.

"Thank you."

"Thanks, *bruh.*"

"No problem."

"EG, did you see who your boy Adrian came with?"

"Yeah, man!"

"If I would have bet you on that, I would have lost big time."

ॐঔৎৎৼ

Fiona's beauty stupefied many of the men who were in attendance at the party. She was strikingly fine-looking for the occasion. Her dark skin, almond-shaped eyes, and nice figure on a strong frame of western Africa brought her covetous attention. It also caused a few men to receive scolding elbows to their ribcages by their female companions. Even though she was in the company of her own mate, it did not stop the onlookers from taking in the curvaceous measurements in the form-fitting, thigh-length black dress.

"'ey babe, nice party." Fiona complimented the host. "Earl, this is Abayomi Gant. Abayomi, this is *Masseur* Earl Grey."

"Mister Gant." Earl extended his hand in receipt of Abayomi's handshake, which had a soft and weak grip.

"Mister Grey, I'm one of your biggest fans. I follow you on Facebook, Twitter and I've tried to friend you on LinkedIn." Abayomi spoke with an African accent.

"Thank you."

"I'm a Marketing and Branding manager at Home Depot. I've read your book. As a matter of fact, it's on my desk at work. I've been telling Fee . . ." Abayomi grabbed Fiona around the waist-cinching her closer to him, letting his hand rest low on her hip – more on gripping her upper cheek. Unnoticeable to Earl, Fiona tensed up. ". . . I'm going to be like you one day, then she can stop talking so much about you and she can hype me up."

Before speaking, Earl assessed the closeness of the couple standing in front of him. "Your goal Abayomi should be to be *a better you*, not a better me. From what I can see and hear, you're on your way."

"Right, that's what I meant. Thanks." Abayomi explained.

"It was nice meeting you. Thanks for coming, Fiona. Excuse me." Earl walked away not sure just what he was feeling; envied, played, or regret.

At that moment, there was a pang in Earl's heart. The self-induced numbness was wearing off. The reality of him having a penchant for someone who didn't appear to see him the same way clinched and twisted at his sentiment.

It's when he thinks he's past love, is when he meets his last love.

By the end of the night, Earl would ask Fiona for the key to his house and he would make arrangements for her to come and pick up her belongings. In his mind, he resolved to maintain an amicable friendship, but on a less closeness arrangement - going back to his original terms and conditions of being a 6FF.

Fiona pushed her way out of Abayomi's grasp. She was torn between going after Earl to explain or letting it keep until later. Her choice was to go to the open bar to get another cocktail of Grey Goose and Red Bull

❧❧❧❧❧

The mingling of party guests had settled into small cliques. Business partners had gathered to discuss among themselves. There appeared to be speculation about a hot topic that brought them together by their dinner party host.

This was Adrian's first time visiting Earl's luxurious home. Even though he lives in a swank high-rise condo, in the ritzy Midtown-Bulkhead part of Atlanta, he was quite envious of his friend's level of success and eclectic design taste.

Adrian regaled himself to survey the spans of the wide-open floor plan to recognize a few familiar faces. He became a wallflower, nursing some Scotch whiskey. His plus one guest Alex returned from the bar with a refreshed margarita over ice with sugar on the rim of the glass.

"Your friend has a beautiful home. And it's just him, huh?" Alex asked.

"I guess," Adrian responded with a tone of **coveting**.

"What do you mean, you guess? I thought you two were best friends."

"That doesn't mean that I know who he's sleeping with."

"Who said anything about who he's sleeping with? Adrian, are you all right?"

"Yes, I'm fine."

"Who's that woman that your friend was just talking to? She's **very** pretty."

"She's a friend of *his*."

"And the guy she's with? They look like a nice couple."

"I don't know **him**." Adrian felt a sense of vengeful satisfaction seeing Fiona in the company of a man **instead of** Earl.

"You've been looking over at **them or** her most of the night. Did he steal her away from you?"

"What!? No!"

"So then why don't you pay more attention to me?" Alex rested a hand gently on Adrian's forearm.

"I apologize. I hadn't realized that I had been neglectful."

"Well, you have. Now, this might not be the appropriate place and all, but I was hoping you could give me some professional advice."

"If I can."

"Lately, I uh, haven't really been able to get in the mood – if you know what I mean."

"In the mood?"

"You know, *in the mood.*" Alex then squeezed Adrian's forearm to emphasize the point.

Still not **grasping** the specific intention of the open-ended implied question, Adrian responded pragmatically and most professionally.

"Oh well; that's not uncommon for **people** these days. Especially women who are head of households or single women in highly stressful careers, find it hard to uh, relax. I **read** where **healthcare** groups and university researchers signed an open letter to the U.S. **FDA**, urging the government agency to approve the first-ever drug to treat the most commonly reported form of female sexual dysfunction, hypoactive sexual desire disorder (HSDD) or low sexual desire." Adrian went on as if he were giving a lecture on **sexual dysfunction**.

Earl walked up and interrupted the session.

"Hello, Adrian. Are you **and your friend** enjoying yourselves?" Earl asked.

"Yes," Adrian answered for the two of them. "Earl, this is Alexandria Dancer. Alexandria, our host Earl Grey."

"Why so formal, man? I'm Earl." He shook hands with the almost mirror reflection of Adrian, only prettier. **Earl noted her firm handshake.**

"Nice to meet you. Most people call me Alex." Out of habit, she quickly reached **into** her purse and handed Earl one of her business cards. "I'm an event planner. Who do you use for your functions?"

"Um, my business manager usually handles that for me. If you like, I can introduce you to her."

"I'd like that." Alex gleefully replied. "Your home is lovely."

"Thank you."

"It's a lot of room for just one person."

"What are you **doing** with this **entire** house?" Adrian questioned.

"**I'm living** in it." Earl frankly replied.

In that instance, the clanging sound of silverware against a crystal glass alerted the attention of the **guests.** Earl's business manager, AT was in the center of the **foyer** holding the stemware. She announced; "Attention everyone, if you will follow me downstairs to the media room. Thank you."

Sixteen – The Bottom of the Barrel

"Help those who would be helped; teach those who would be taught. But don't waste your time with those who have no intention to change." – Bishop Dale C. Bronner

The media room has a dozen built-in theatre seats that filled quickly, leaving the three seats down the front which were reserved. The overflow sat on rented folding chairs. At the front of the room are a leather sectional sofa and a couple of lounge chairs where a few selected guests and Earl took their seats.

Earl's business manager stood in front of the 75" Class 4k television screen.

"Again, thank you all for coming tonight. The wonderful dinner was only part of why you were invited. The other is to announce the premiere of a new program on CNN and you just might recognize someone you know." AT introduced before clicking the remote to start a video to play and taking her seat next to Earl.

The room's backlight dimmed while the TV screen brightened. A backdrop of a black and white split screen came into view. A voiceover came through the overhead surround sound speakers in the theatre room. *"Not everything is as simple as black and white. There is also The Grey Side, with Earl Grey."* The image of Earl Grey appeared at the dividing point of the opposing two colors.

The in-house viewing guests applaud, many of them expressed exasperation or surprise. The video continued to play.

"Hello, I'm Earl Grey, and welcome to The Grey Side. The median wage of the bottom ninety percent of Americans is lower today than it was three decades ago, adjusted for inflation, even though the economy is twice as large. Almost all the gains from that growth have gone to the top one percent of Americans. As a result, the middle class doesn't have the buying power necessary for buoyant growth.

"A recent study by the Institute of Assets and Social Policy showed that the lack of inherited wealth is one of the major causes of African-American's inability to increase their net worth. Because each generation starts from 'scratch' or at the bottom of the barrel with no assets, it takes them longer to establish a solid financial foundation.

"To talk about the state of the economy and its lack to maintain financial buoyancy is my guest today Cynthia Anita-Simone Henderson, founder of CASH Flow Management a financial services agency and best-selling author of 'Act Your Wage: Live Within Your Means.'

"Welcome, Cynthia."

"Hello Earl and thank you for having me."

"Recently you published a blog that addressed the bottom percentile of our social-economic status. Calling them the working poor, the disenfranchised – whatever. The title of the blog was 'The Bottom of the Barrel.' Now I'm no economist, but you presented an interesting perspective that even I could understand and identify with. If I can introduce a little bit of it and let you follow up, is that okay?"

"Sure."

"In your somewhat controversial blog, instead of pointing out the reason for the disparity between the top one percent of Americans who supposedly own forty percent of the nation's wealth and the bottom ninety-nine percent wage earners in America; you examine the

condition of what you call the 'bottom of the barrel dwellers' and why some of them are there due to their own doing or not doing," Earl concluded.

"Yes. I came to look at this group of people in the United States once I saw a comment from one of my Facebook friends, Andre Hughes, Servant at Powered by Action. The comment was on a depiction of men like crabs in a barrel. Andre's comment was; "They are stuck in a fixed, not growth mentality."

"Cynthia, is this the same ole' hater crabs-in-the-barrel mentality that we've heard about?"

"Not exactly – the mentality that has prevailed since it was first coined by Filipino writer and feminist, Ninotchka Rosca has quite naturally evolved. The Crab Mentality describes an 'if I can't have it, neither can you'-way of thinking. Especially amongst people of color, that mentality is still perpetuated."

"Let me stop you right here," Earl interjected "because I have something to say about the crab-in-the-barrel condition as you and I have debated before. I say that this whole analogy is based on a falsehood. For one, real crabs in a barrel are not in their natural habitat. They are put in a foreign environment, and we say that their reaction or response to an attempt to escape is wrong. The myth is that the crabs on the bottom hate on the crab that's closest to getting out, and in response, they try to pull it down. Why isn't the top crab viewed as uplifting and willing to pull up the other crabs? I'm sorry, I don't want to get off-topic here, but I'm passionate about this which is why I invited you on today's show."

"No, no, you're correct Earl. In our society, it's easier to promote the negative stereotype of the crab-in-the-barrel mentality, than how you see it. The negative mindset is easier to take hold. This can be traced back to the basis of the Willie Lynch Letter, the house versus the field slave, and the Haves and the Have Nots. Though historically there is evidence to the contrary of the 'hater, pull them back' mentality. One of my favorite quotes is from Mary McLeod Bethune who said; 'You may climb, but remember to lift others as you climb.'"

"I like that. I would imagine those words would have encouraged the likes of Harriet Tubman and those involved in the whole Underground Railroad Movement."

"Possibly. . ."

இ-ஞ-ஒ-ஒ

Fiona nudged **Abayomi who was** sitting next to her; "'arriet Tubman is one of my role models."

Abayomi looked at her quizzically; "How can she be your role model, **if** she's dead?"

At that moment; in all of her mind, body, and soul Fiona yearned to be sitting **down front** next to Earl.

இ-ஞ-ஒ-ஒ

Cynthia Henderson continued. "But here's how the crabs-in-the-barrel mentality has evolved to adapt in today's world. It's no longer dominated by the hater crabs."

"Right, you've identified some new crabs-in-the-barrel."

"Yes, these new crabs have evolved to survive **in the barrel.** *Here's an observation that I've made over many years of financial counseling. There is this first generation of successful individuals. Whether they are the first ones to go to college and graduate or to get a corporate job and earn a salary wage instead of being paid by the hour – these first generationers are the out-of-the-barrel crabs* **or maybe still on the climb.***

"Now, by the old definition; there are Hater Crabs – **'underachievers'** *the 'fixed crabs' that become jealous or filled with a sense of self-loathing or low self-esteem, so they find a way to pull that person back down by undermining the success of the out-of-the-barrel*

crab. Hater crabs will wish you the best, and then hate when you have it. The out-of-the-barrel crab receives sniping comments like 'you think you're better or smarter than everybody.'"

"Right. So how does the Hater Crab have a financial impact?"

"They don't directly. But they could cause the out-of-the-barrel crab to lose momentum and not reach its full potential so as not to make the hater crab feel left behind. To your point Earl, let me quickly speak to those crabs that do directly affect the financial conditions of the out-of-the-barrel crabs and in my opinion contribute to increasing the number of those in the bottom of the barrel and to remain there."

"Please do, because I found this enlightening."

"Okay. These other crabs I have heard about from my clients when I work with them to get their finances on the right track of prosperity."

"Excuse me; did you just use the P-word?" Earl questioned, causing Cynthia to chuckle.

"Yes, I did. Prosperity has gotten a bad rap because of the misuse and tarnish of some institutions, which shall remain nameless. My definition of prosperity is living beneath or within your means. Someone is prosperous if they can pay their bills and have something left over to put away for savings. A person is prosperous when they can care for their needs and have enough to comfortably help others without hurting themselves. Prosperity is NOT the accumulation of stuff that someone has told you that you have to have to be somebody."

"Nice. Thank you for that. So back to these other crabs."

"So, I did not make these crabs up. I just identified them and if you don't know some of these bottom-of-the-barrel crabs, then they may be you."

Earl chuckled; "Well I hope not."

"First, you have your Pincher Crabs – they will nickel, dime and dollar you to debt. They keep the change from purchase when you send them to the store. They will send by you to buy from the dollar menu, with exactly a dollar, with no more to cover the taxes. The Pincher crabs smoke, but never buy a pack of cigarettes because they're constantly bumming off of you."

"Oh, I can see the Pincher Crab," Earl interjected.

"We all can, but we don't see how they're slowly pinching away at *our* money by having you buy a pack of cigarettes quicker than you *normally* would have to."

"Okay, okay I see."

"Next is the Puller Crabs – they are a bit more aggressive, inconsiderate, and chronic. They buy what they want and beg for what they need. They are about **begging** to the point of keeping others from getting ahead or **causing** them to fall behind. **They get people to cosign for a loan and then they default on it.** The Puller **Crab** knows when you get paid."

"**Now** that's serious."

"But Earl, there is one more crab and the worst of them all - **the** Grabber Crab. This crab is a freeloader and a thief. A Grabber Crab will take as much of your generosity that is offered and more if **it** isn't enough to satisfy their greedy needs. When all is gone they will simply move on."

"To be fair Cynthia, you aren't advocating that we don't help our fellow man, are you? I'm pretty sure a lot of charity and religious groups would be in opposition to that line of thinking. Actually, I heard something that has stayed on my heart which was; 'the blessed of us are here for the rest of us.'"

"Not at all – in fact, there is a scripture that says 'let your giving be with discretion.' I'm not saying **to** not be charitable or giving, not at all.

This may sound selfish, but in the financial world, you need to be securing yourself before you can help others."

"Sort of like what the flight attendants say about putting the air mask on yourself, before trying to help the person sitting next to you." Earl pointed out.

"Exactly."

"So do you have any tips for dealing with these pincher, puller, and grabber crabs without feeling guilty?"

*"The first thing is to identify and recognize the type of crab that you have in your life. They're sometimes hidden in plain sight. They can be your closest friends and even a family member. Here are my four rules about giving and helping others. **Give only what you can afford to lose. Give without expectations. Give within your means. Don't give until it hurts you or hurts your relationship with someone else.** And Earl, these work in helping those who've made it out of the barrel and to help them stay up. I have unsolicited testimonials from many of my clients. One of my clients shared with me their way of saying no when a relative comes to them asking for money. He tells them; 'I'd rather you be mad at me for not lending you the money than for me being mad at you for not paying me back.'"*

"Thank you Cynthia Henderson of CASH Flow Management for sharing and being on the show today."

"Thank you for having me. It was my pleasure."

"After the break; 'a better you make a better we' message from The Grey Side."

📖 📖 📖 📖 📖

Applause and cheers, hooping and a few whistles came from Earl's media room viewing audience. Donald, one of his business partners who was sitting behind him; placed both of his hands on Earl's shoulders and shook him with **congratulatory** jubilation. Those who were in arms reach of Earl gave pats on his back. The CNN promotion spots ended and **Earl's image** reappeared on the television screen.

"Welcome back to The Grey Side. As a child growing up, I didn't need anything. My parents provided a roof over my head, food, and clothing. When my father died, my mother continued to make sure I had the necessities of life. When it came to things that I wanted; well, my mother did what she could to see that I had a few of those too.

"I remember getting my first G.I. Joe Action Figure. You couldn't tell me anything – I was the happiest little boy on the block. But that didn't last long. That's because Hasbro came out with the G.I. Joe with the Kung Fu grip. Then came the African American G.I. Joe with life like-hair, then the talking G.I. Joe and I told my mother I just had to have them. My mother's initial response was "No, we can't afford it" and some absurdity about 'money not growing on trees.'

*"She then came to her senses and **her** 'no' changed to 'maybe we can put them on **your** birthday/Christmas wish list.' My mother said if I couldn't wait until then, I could do extra chores around the house to increase my allowance. That led me to work opportunities outside of the house raking yards and shoveling snow off neighbors' walks to earn money.*

*"Growing up, I didn't know **about any** great divide between the rich and the poor – the Have's and Haves Nots, - the Top One Percent and the 99 Percent or the above the rim and bottom of the barrel dwellers. I was taught to get what you wanted in life that you had to get up, get out and work. Pay for what you want. Somewhere in the Bible, it says 'that if any would not work, neither should he eat.' My mother will be proud that I quoted the Bible.*

*"**Anyway**, I'm also going to quote the tempting Temptation's Apostle Paul from the book of the Joneses; on a solution to our debt-ridden society. 'Now listen, if you see something you want and you know you can't afford it, the very next thing for you to do is start saving towards*

it. The Joneses have been a downfall for many persons, you see. So people take my advice and let the Joneses be.'

*"For whatever reason that you are finding yourself in a proverbial barrel, you must start by adjusting your motionless mindset and get a move on. Get out of your comfort zone and stretch your capabilities and follow your God-given gift and talent – your purpose. Most importantly is that you start the climb. **Whoever** is trying to bring you down is already beneath you. Don't allow them to. Stand firm, stay strong, stay **focused** and stay up. I'm Earl Grey; see you next time from The Grey Side."*

❧❦❧❦

After the viewing of *The Grey Side*, Earl received more congratulatory responses from his guests. A server came around with a tray of Rosa Regale sparkling wine to toast their friend and new celebrity. As the night's event came to an end a few visitors stayed behind. To offset the effects of the night of alcohol drinking, the guests are offered assorted tins of Garrett's popcorn and Café Du Monde chicory coffee.

One particular guest wished she could stay overnight in the room prepared for her. But Fiona could not because she had picked Abayomi up from his mother's house and drove them to the dinner event. Earl requested from Fiona her key to the house. She regrettably relinquished it, not wishing to make a scene. From her room, she took only the mink fur teddy bear from atop the queen bed. Fiona left Earl's goodbye hugging arms with a sullen attitude. *"Bonne nuit mon ami,"* she conceded.

Adrian gave Earl a man hug with a fist pound on his back, genuinely happy for his accomplishment. Alex gave Earl a deliberate pressing thigh and gliding raised knee across his crotch when she hugged him. "Call me." She whispered into his ear.

Deshaun, Vera, Bradley, and Mama Maria were standing in the foyer ready to leave. Deshaun and Earl exchanged a bro-hug. With teary eyes, Vera joined the embrace. **Mama** Maria unaware of the reason for the show of sentiment **turned to** Bradley **who** hunched his shoulders.

ॐॐॐॐ

MONTH LATER

The Fulton County Medical Examiner's **Office** released the identity of a naked woman **found fatally stabbed several times in the back - in NE Atlanta.** The body **identified as** Kendra Reynolds, **in her** mid-thirties, was found in the Old Fourth Ward, in front of a home in the 600 block of Boulevard Street NE. Her body was discovered **Sunday** around 3 a.m., according to Atlanta police. Reynolds's body had several stab wounds and was dumped in a barrel. **The** death **is** still under investigation.

Not released to the public, was that the victim had her head shoved inside a Michael Kors purse and had a $2 bill stuffed in her mouth.

"THAT'S ALL FOLKS!"

Author's Note

I wanted to write something with an enlightening purpose to the reader for them to improve and maintain their financial footing in their climb to prosperity and stability. *Stay up!*

"Act Your Wage – Live Within Your Means"

1. Live beneath your means. [NOW; needs over wants]
2. Cut expenses. [review income vs. expenses]
3. Create additional income. [Stir up your gift]
4. Utilize free money (employer's matching 401K).
5. Tithe [The blessed of us are here for the rest of us.]
6. Pay yourself.
7. Insure yourself (for your next generation).
8. Establish an emergency fund. [Six months' worth]
9. Diversify
10. Create separate savings account for other purposes.
11. Loan money with interest or education.

About the Author

LAWRENCE CHRISTOPHER is the author of a combined eight books and novellas, most notably his Mick Hart mysteries, the first of which, *All About Mary* was a best seller.

www.ingramcontent.com/pod-product-compliance
Lightning Source LLC
Chambersburg PA
CBHW051850170626
46807CB00003B/1409